The Ghostwriter & the Muse

Building a Bridge From the Edge of Eternity

*To Mike and Lisa —
With love & best wishes —
Madeline Westbrook*

A NOVEL

MADELINE MAXINE WESTBROOK

M.A. NEVETSON
PUBLISHERS

HOUSTON, TEXAS

The Ghostwriter and the Muse
Building a Bridge From the Edge of Eternity

© 2005 by Madeline Maxine Westbrook

For information address:

M.A. NEVETSON
PUBLISHERS

M.A. Nevetson Publishers
1127 Eldridge Pkwy., Ste. 300-371
Houston, Texas USA 77077

Please contact the author if you would like
to interview, plan an article, or if you
need additional information.

www.madelinewrites.com

Classification: General Fiction

ISBN: 0-9760445-0-1

Cover design, illustrations and electronic production:
The Marion Group / www.marion.com

FIRST EDITION

Printed in the United States of America.

To Past and Future Bridge Builders

To our solid foundation:
Bill with love beyond words.
He's Husband, Dad and Grandpa to the clan.

Our sons and their families:
Bill II and Susan:
their children, Jennifer and Liz.
Steve and Ginger:
their children, Chris and Katie.
Douglas and Lisa:
their children, Aaron, Daniel and Abigail.

To the Reader

THIS BOOK EXISTS because it was the dying wish of a young lawyer. He wanted to write his own book but, as his illness progressed, it became evident he would not reach his writing goals.

Instead, he began making a different set of plans, secretly talking to his mother about writing novels for him after his death. He wanted to try an experiment. He planned to build a bridge from eternity back to his loved ones. He wanted to do it through writing, music, and nature.

The young man was our son, my husband's and mine. The year was 1994.

I think now, it was his love for his family that made him want to stay connected. Maybe he was trying to lessen the loss for all of us. Whether it was an actual plan in the beginning or some way to avoid facing death, I'll never know. None of us will ever know his true reasons.

What I do know is that his thoughts turned into powerful forces in my heart. Our son introduced me to a new way of living, a new way of looking at life. I hope this book is what he expected it to be.

This book is a novel. Names, places and times have been changed, although the novel has been inspired and adapted from true events that happened during our son's illness and after he died. I've written of personal, yet specific moments that have occurred throughout ten difficult years of grief, and at times, seemingly unbearable loss. While trudging my life roads, searching for the bridge he hoped to build, I came across fascinating adventures and spiritual quests I'd not thought possible. I learned to believe in miracles.

How could I, now a seventy-one-year old woman with minimal college education, follow my son's plans for me to study writing, listen for special musical messages and look for signs in nature that he thought he would make happen?

I was the first to doubt the seemingly impossible idea. Pushing myself, I studied and remained open during those difficult years. I learned that unexpected happenings often lead to breakthroughs and discoveries from unknown realms.

My awareness grew as encounters with bagpipers and their music, the inspired lessons of my writing instructors and mentors, and extraordinary signs from nature's bounty joined together to send me wonders from a Great Source. Sometimes called upon, but other times unsought, treasures that touched my heart were shared at just the right time and place. Our son in his wisdom gathered a talented group of ethereal "engineers" to construct his bridge.

The Ghostwriter and the Muse is a gift to readers who wish to believe in and accept more than the ordinary. It's my wish that others will find the hope that can come with tragic loss.

The writing years have opened the doors of my mind. I've learned to do the incredible. My belief in unending life is firm. I've learned to cherish the experiences of serendipity and synchronicity.

Most of all I've learned to look for a special kind of divine order in life and death.

I know there is a purpose in my life and for this little book. Call it what you want, I felt God's love guiding each word. No matter the reason you've picked up *The Ghostwriter and the Muse*, I hope it will prove to be a source of inspiration.

– Madeline Maxine Westbrook
Fall 2005

Into the Unknown

"Faith is our direct link to universal wisdom,
reminding us that we know more
than we have heard or read or studied –
that we have only to look, listen,
and trust the love and wisdom
of the Universal Spirit
working through us all."

Dan Millman – *The Laws of Spirit*

I WALKED INTO THE eighth-floor hospital room and looked at my sleeping son. His body was too tall for the bed. His feet were resting on top of the footboard of the bed. The room was cold and dim and the curtains were open enough to reveal that the deep windowsill behind them was stacked high with books and audiotape albums. The radio was softly playing Mozart. I felt a chill and slipped into the sweater that was tied around my neck. Get well cards were piled on the area by the sink, half of them still unopened. A child's drawing was taped with surgical tape on the opposite wall so it could be seen from the bed.

A briefcase full of legal files sat on the floor. Next to it, another briefcase held writing projects in various stages of completion. On the bedside table, more legal pads and a coffee mug full of pencils and pens. A blood pressure cuff loosely folded and almost falling off the table left little room for items doctors or nurses might need. The bedside drawer was pulled out and used as an extension for table space. Toilet items and food saved from meal trays, candy bars, note pads, his address book, wallet and a small telephone file overflowed and made it impossible to close the drawer. Our son's room was his legal office, his writing studio and a library full of books. The telephone shared his bed. I saw him making every effort to be surrounded by his working life. The hospital room had been transformed into an office. His law associates had little hope of his coming back to work; but still, he called and kept in touch with the office and his clients. He was sick, but working. Although hopeful, he was fearfully and hesitantly planning to die. It was the greatest of all great enigmas.

I looked through the audiocassette tape albums and knew the messages from the messengers: Richard Bach, Dr. Norman Vincent Peale, Rev. Howard Caesar, Og Mandino, Dr. Anthony Robbins, Dr. Wayne Dyer, Dan Millman, Father Leo Booth, Bernie Siegel MD, Larry Dossey MD, Zig Ziglar, and Vince Lombardi, on and on his list continued.

I saw the tiny book *As a Man Thinketh* by James Allen. Books by Carl Jung and Albert Einstein. The ever-present Bible. The young man in the hospital bed, Neil Galloway, was searching for meaning.

Our family had listened to motivational and spiritual speakers for years. Life 101 as taught by the best speakers and writers, "You must be willing to do whatever it takes to make your dreams come true." The tapes were part of our family discussions. Now they were part of his plan to overcome his illness. He would write books and go on the speaking circuit. He certainly had the stage presence and was a gifted speaker. We each held to the idea of his overcoming his illness but, as I looked at him, I wondered how this nightmare could disappear. I could feel time slipping away.

I refused to think about it for the thousandth time.

My attention was drawn to another pile of books and magazines. They were about fishing and outdoors. Mostly about fishing. He was most at home in the outdoors when he was fishing. I noticed his prized antique book *Fisherman's Luck* by Henry Van Dyke. Neil had found it at a book sale when he was just eleven years old.

Please God, let him go fishing again with his dad and brothers.

Neil Galloway, our thirty-seven-year old son, opened his eyes and turned my way. I made an effort to overlook the shine on his bronze-colored head and the horseshoe suture marks made by the neurosurgeon. Barely healed, the surgical scars were there to mark where the scalpel had peeled back the skin on his head before drilling was done to open his skull. Arches of dark blue-black pencil marks just above his ears and on top of his head, sketched there by a radiation specialist, marked where his brain had been repeatedly given radiation treatment.

Neil smiled. His sky-blue eyes twinkled in sharp contrast with his bald, medically road-mapped head. There had never been anything dull in his thoughts, body, or life. Not even after the draining physical abuse caused by his surgery, cancer treatments and the severe pain he continued to endure for months after. I wondered if we would ever see his blond hair again.

"Hi, Mom. I've been listening to music and have tried the radio station once or twice. I don't know about this. At first I get excited and then I get depressed. How can I be so dumb as to think we can make plans for after our deaths?" He smiled weakly, still revealing his sense of humor. "Let's try the 70's station." He reached to change the dial on his small portable radio.

"Fact is, let's do it this way: if you die before me, you send me messages on the 70's station. You can learn to know the songs and music I really like. You learn to appreciate my generation's music, okay? And if I go first, I'll come to you on your easy listening and classical stations. Whoever is left standing will get to search for the messages given in the music we like best. Whoever's here gets to act normal. Heather and the kids would not understand me being tuned in to your oldies, and I have a feeling everyone would think you were cracked if you went around listening to rock and light rock all day. How could you explain you were listening for a message from your dead son?"

I walked to the window and flung the curtains open wide. Oh, how I wished sunshine would blast forth and brighten his room. Rather, another cold gray day.

"Stop it. Neil, stop talking that way. We both must be crazy. You can plan all you want but you're going to be all right. You'll recover from the radiation illness. You'll be up and out of here as soon as they get the swelling and headaches under control."

I couldn't help wondering if his thinking had changed. I told myself it hadn't, not really. Our son, the attorney, always thinking way ahead of his peers. As an adult, he'd retained the grand and vivid imagination he had as a child. Enthusiastically reaching for more education, he enrolled in writing classes where he wrote fantasy and poetry. Legal thrillers and horror. Humor and sports stories. Fishing tales. Science fiction and fantasy. Mystical stories. The one about a bagpiper in the Texas Hill Country was a favorite.

But this secret experiment, building this seemingly impossible bridge from eternity to earth, was clearly original. Unusual, yes, but that is Neil. Who is he? A sensitive family man. An athlete, a nature lover, a fisherman. A dreamer. An attorney, yet also accepted to medical school. An inventive cook who grew vegetables and flowers in his garden during every season. A writer. More than that? Certainly not a Houdini or a medium. Not a psychic. A thinking and planning man. Planning in the courtroom and in life. A religious, spirit-filled man. A Renaissance man, of sorts.

I busied myself picking up candy and fast food wrappers that had missed the trashcan. M&Ms and cheese crackers. Junk food. Neil's room never had hospital smells. Today, it smelled of chocolate and shaving lotion.

I pulled my chair over to the bed and sat down. Neil stretched, reached for his robe at the foot of the bed and put it on. He pulled himself up and slowly walked to the window. *He's lost weight.* His tall 6-ft., 2-inch frame looked frail, yet I knew he weighed 170 pounds. How can a person look frail at 170 pounds? I remember his days as a football lineman when he weighed 225. Throwing the shot put and javelin had kept his arm and leg muscles as large as a weight lifter's.

"Mom, I ask myself about this musical plan. I think we'd best not tell anyone the truth of it just yet. At least not while I'm alive. I don't want to deal with scrutiny. I know there are folks who feel mystical things and have them happen at times, but let's not talk about it to the family yet. When it comes time, it'll be easy for them to understand what we're doing and why. They'll want to join us. Especially if something happens to get their attention. And it will."

He turned away and looked into space.

Thoughtfully, he said, "I believe life is mystical and everlasting for those who seek the Forces that make it so. I know there is something about the way sounds resonate with us. I think we really could be like E.T., Mom, and communicate from wherever we are."

Looking back toward the window, he drew a big breath and hunched his back slightly. I thought he might be getting faint. But, then he stood straight again. I was glad his back was to me.

"Neil, we'll be together wherever we are." I tried to keep my voice steady and calm. "We will teach the family how we do it. We will do whatever it takes."

He turned again, cautiously, and looked straight at me.

"And my kids and Heather, Mom. What about Patrick, Kellie and Heather?" Tears came to his eyes. "I don't want to die, Mom. Will they try to stay in touch with me, too?"

In the silence of the room we, at the same moment, turned toward the radio and paused a second to turn up the volume.

"Listen, Mom. The radio. Mariah Carey is singing 'Hero.' I really like that song. Music has a way of helping us deal with our difficulties. How is it we hear what we need to hear? What message does the music send? And why do we hear it when we need it the most? Maybe it's the rhythm of love and its possibilities. All I know is it helps with my fear and sanity."

Standing strong and tall he said again, but this time resolutely, "Mom, I don't want to die."

I couldn't talk. I walked over and reached for his hand and held it tight. There was nothing to do but listen.

"Mom, I had the strangest dream last night. I dreamed I was in the movie *Ghost*. I was sliding through doors and could see everyone, like the guy in the movie. Except he left and I didn't. I never did. I was always there on the other side, sending messages from the bridge. Do you remember when you and Dad were raising us kids? You told me and my two brothers if we could dream it, say it or write it, we could do it? Did you really think it was possible? Do you think it now?"

I couldn't answer. I was sick to my stomach as I listened to our wonderful, accomplished thirty-seven-year old son, now a man, remembering his childhood and the beliefs his father and I tried to instill in all our sons. I wanted him to plan his experiment, to dream. I wanted it desperately and I didn't care if it sounded crazy. I wanted to help.

It was all we had.

The Muse-i-cal Message

*For centuries, the dead have been provided
with the sonic tools for the spiritual journey
to the next life through prayer and song.
Music and sound weave a magic carpet
for the soul's journey.*

Don Campbell – *The Mozart Effect*™

I DROVE AS FAST AS I
dared. It was another evening heading home from the
hospital and a way to keep myself busy and moving.
If I slowed down, I might let the nightmare catch me.
Days were spent with Neil in the hospital and going
back and forth home. Nights meant wanting to avoid
the phone and talking on it anyway. There were his
brothers and the grandparents and Heather, his wife,
who couldn't bear the nightmare and spent time trying
to shield their children. I knew it was difficult but
what was going on? Nothing felt normal in our family.
Travis, our oldest son, and family were calling from
Iowa and, for once, I was glad of the distance. I didn't
have to face them. But Austin, our youngest, lived
near our home and was in fear that God, the Great
Protector, was going to take his big brother who had
always been his earthly protector. Heather, the faithful

protector. She was living inside her disbelief and deep sadness while steadfastly building the strength she needed to care for their two children, Patrick and Kellie. My Dan, the father of our sons, living in silence except when he erupted in rage. Rage at life and everything connected with Neil's illness. Neil, his best friend and business partner. His attorney and weekly fishing buddy. His pride and joy.

A cancer hospital may help to heal but it can be seen at times as a killer. Maybe, in some ways, it kills the family as it works to heal the patient. True in our family. We were dying. Everyone made excuses why not to go. Everyone but me. No need to ask why. I was beginning to see us become a dysfunctional family, but certainly not because of drinking, drugs, or any of the usual reasons. The cog of our family circle was dismantling. We were falling apart.

For me, it was easier to be at the hospital with Neil than with the family. I clung to the moments we had and pretended everything would be okay. I wasn't ready to accept otherwise. And at this place and time, it seemed we were bonding again as a newborn and parent. In some strange way, we were beginning life anew, although, it was so very different. He was raising me, he was teaching me and I was growing up in his ways. It was a beginning of an ending and it was those plans for a new beginning that kept us looking for dreams of a future, whatever and however irrational they were. There were no nightmares when we were planning. The nightmare came when I stepped out of his hospital room.

Dreams of an unknown future were between the two of us when we were in his small hospital room that became a classroom. I didn't want to leave. I wanted to stay and I wanted him to live forever. I lingered a while at the door looking, snapping and unsnapping the flap on my purse. I slowly buttoned my sweater, as I walked to the hospital parking lot and finally made it to my car. There was a full moon, a harvest moon, beginning to rise in the eastern sky. Looking at the moon, I remembered the little verse I'd once loved to recite. My grandma taught me; "I see the moon and the moon sees me. God bless the moon and God bless me." I said the verse again; this time I asked God to bless Neil.

It was nearly dark as I drove speedily toward home. I was in my great race with the nightmare. It was as close as it had been. I didn't want to leave our hospital classroom and I didn't want to admit his condition was changing. Neil had changed colors. I tried hard not to look but there was no doubt. His bald head looked puffy. The doctor had said it was a reaction to something.

Sometimes when I looked at my son I thought about other patients in the hospital.

Female cancer patients wore wigs or pretty hats and scarves to cover the damage done by the treatment or surgery. They could distinguish themselves from each other. If there were distinguishing features on the men's heads, they were the scars on the heads of male patients who had brain surgery.

Racing with the nightmare, I stopped at the store to pick up groceries for dinner. As I entered the store, I heard Mariah Carey begin to sing "Hero" on the overhead sound system. I walked to the grocery carts and slowly pulled one from the long, neat string of carts in the lobby at the front of the store. I admired the orderly look of the carts and thought of my desire for our normal lives. The carts were perfectly in place, one after another. Would we ever be the same?

I looked at the pay phone on the opposite side of the lobby and pushed my cart to the phone. I stopped, stood, and listened to the song.

I searched my purse for a quarter and called home.

"Dan, I can't come home tonight. I want to sit awhile longer with Neil. He looks worse. I'm going back to the hospital."

"Should I come, Marion?"

"Not unless I call, or if you feel you want to come. Don't you think you should get some rest? Didn't you say you had a busy day scheduled at the veterinary clinic?"

"Yeah, I do but I'd meet you at the hospital if you needed me."

"I know you would, Dan. I promise I'll call if his condition changes.

It was a calm conversation. I knew Dan found it difficult to make more than one hospital visit a day. He'd rather take Austin to dinner and in doing so, I wasn't worried about Dan being alone. I knew I could count on Dan.

"I think it'd be great if you come by before you go to the veterinary clinic in the morning. I'll tell Neil. He'll be happy to see you. I just want to be with him tonight. I love you Dan."

"Thank God for our marriage." I said out loud as I

climbed into my minivan and turned on the roads that led back to the hospital and Neil's room on the eighth floor. Room 812 was the place that had taken my heart and forced it into a tight grip.

The closer I got to the medical center the more the nightmare faded. By the time I walked into Neil's room, it had almost disappeared. He wasn't sleeping and the radio was on.

"I couldn't go home, son. Let's talk some more about your thoughts and plans. I heard "Hero" at the grocery store and had to come back. Are you too tired to talk? If you are, I'll sit and read one of your books."

"Mom, I heard it, too, and I mentally asked you to come back. Look, I wrote down the time and the station. When did you hear it?"

I looked at his notes and realized the grocery store was tuned into the same easy listening station. We heard the same song at the same time.

"I got your message, Neil. I didn't know it at the time but now I think we might've had our first break through."

Our smiles were correspondingly wide and happy.

"Let's talk more, Mom. I'm not sleepy. I've written more about our experiment. Want to read it?"

"You bet your life I do, Neil."

"Yes, Mom, that is exactly what we are doing."

He smiled. We settled in for the next phase of the plan.

Neil wrote on a yellow legal pad, one of many stacked beside his bed. I kept the thought to ask him if I could read his notebooks. I wanted to see what he had been writing. Not now. Later, I told myself.

He said, "These are the things we need to do. You'll need to enroll in my writing class at the university, Mom. Don't tell anyone who you are. My professor has so many students he won't connect us unless you tell him. Don't tell him at first. Maybe there will be another time . . . later.

"Why don't you take this lecture series about serendipity now?

"And listen to the Jack Boland series on *Jonathan Livingston Seagull*."

Neil stopped reading from his notes. He didn't need them. He knew what he wanted. He said, "Just as well, Mom, do this. You keep all these tapes I have here. Listen to them. Give them to my kids when they are in college or when they'll be interested enough to hear them and get something from the messages. I've learned so much from them. I always thought I would teach my children the important things in life."

He paused and took a deep breath.

"Gather my music cassettes. Listen to the music while you write. Listen to the audiotapes when you are riding to my writing class at the university. Practice knowing what I listen to. Then, turn on the radio. See what happens."

Continuing like the lawyer he'd been, almost demanding, "You are going to need to be open, Mom. You'll need to look and listen for me. In the words, the music. Look for me in nature. In unlikely places. Not just a bird or a rainbow. But a special tree or bird. Maybe Jonathan Seagull. A rainbow at a special time, when you are asking for a sign or when you are not looking for one. Just be open.

"I've been listening to our minister talk about butterflies. First the worm, then it spins the cocoon and then the miracle. Everyone knows about it here on earth. What we've got to do in this situation is spin the cocoon so I can be a miracle. Maybe with angel wings like the butterfly. Maybe not. Maybe like the seed that grows the trees or other plants.

"I've been thinking, Mom. You and I know life goes on. It must. All cultures believe it. Why should it be difficult for us? It shouldn't be hard. We'll just need to change a few beliefs and know we'll connect. We will in many ways. In special ways. I'd like to see it as building a bridge from me back to here. From Eternity. Love can build my bridge. Love will build it to Heather and to Patrick and Kellie and the rest of the family. I'll need your help. You'll teach them how to be receptive. Will you do that for me? Talking about it won't be enough. You write it, Mom and write it so they'll remember me. Think of it. You'll be my Ghostwriter and I'll be your Muse. Always remember, Mom."

In a softer voice Neil said, "Will you promise to remember this stuff? I'm not going to let you forget me, Mom."

He stopped talking and smiled sheepishly. "You know, if anyone heard us talking this way, they'd think we both had brain cancer!"

I answered, wanting to show him I could help carry out the plan, even if it seemed almost a joke to both of us. "Who cares what folks think, Neil. It's your plan. I buy it and we can talk about it as much as you like."

"I know, I know. Maybe it's something to pass the time. Hang in here with me, Mom. I need to make plans. The doctors told me to get my life in order. I'd rather we plan for my afterlife and get that part in order."

He continued, "It'll be a bridge from wherever I am to my Heather and our kids. From eternity to here. It'll go to Heather and our kids and to the rest of the family. They may not buy it, but what if it works? They'll have to believe it, right? Talking about it is not enough. You write it, Mom, and write it so they will remember me."

I thought, "How can I possibly forget this young attorney pleading what might be one of his last cases?" I wondered again what was written on the stack of legal pads he has spent time filling and stacking by his bed.

"One more thing, as far as getting my present day life in order, I'm worried about Heather and the children. They'll need you and Dad. You're going to need to support them in so many ways. Don't forget to go to Kellie's dance recitals and Patrick's soccer games. It tears me in pieces to think I may not be there. I could miss the best years of my life, and the best years of Patrick and Kellie's lives. And Heather, I can't leave her alone. I don't want to do that."

"Neil, it's not necessary to talk about this; but of course, we'd do anything for you and your family, I promise." My heart was splitting; his children were so precious and adored their dad.

How could they grow to adulthood without a father? I wanted to run and scream. This is impossible, it isn't happening to Neil and his family. No, it isn't happening to any of us.

He turned to face the window and said, "Sit awhile longer. I think I'll try to get some rest. Let's talk when I wake up. Okay?"

I wrapped my bright multi-colored sweater around my stooped shoulders and walked over to kiss his cheek. He looked very tired and had a wrinkled brow. I wondered if it had come from another one of his persistent headaches. He shut his eyes and relaxed for a moment, and then he suddenly rose up and began repeating his thoughts again.

"Another thing, Mom, about Patrick and Kellie. They'll grow older and need you. Promise me you and Dad will help Heather raise them and see that they go to college."

"Neil, we'd do anything for your family. You know it."

I gently touched his shoulder and said, "Goodnight, get some rest, Neil. I'll be here when you wake up. Want me to put on some music?"

"Yeah, Mom, play Kenny Loggins, the one about Pooh Corner. The one Travis gave me."

That night Neil and I listened to Kenny Loggins sing the hauntingly beautiful songs he'd recorded for his children. We listened to the healing strains of Mozart, too.

While he was asleep, I tiptoed outside the room and went to the small hospital chapel. I fell on my knees to plead with God. I prayed for a miracle.

When I returned to Neil's room, I was there, listening to the music but my mind was slipping in and out of reality. I secretly wanted to remove one yellow legal pad at a time, without disturbing him, and read the rest of his plans. Not a good idea, I thought. Not now.

What had our family done to deserve this? It was insane to think I could go to the university and learn to write a book while enrolled in the same class Neil was taking. More unrealistic, could we communicate through music and nature? People often make deathbed plans and promises. No matter how irrational, they find that inventive and divine ideas are soothing to breaking hearts and troubled minds.

Dear God, was he losing his mind or was I losing mine? Maybe both.

Folks say death and taxes are real. People make fun of it and joke about it. If it's so, why were we always looking to lessen the blows of the inevitable?

I prayed again, this time asking God to help me find a way to know and be helped by Neil's thoughts about his plan to build a bridge from eternity.

Coming back to reality, I pleaded with God to spare our son's life.

Last Plans

Light shines in the darkness for good men.
A good person will never fail; he will
always be remembered. He is not afraid of
receiving bad news; his faith is strong,
and he trusts in the Lord.

— Psalms 113: 4, 7

IN MID-OCTOBER, THE entire family was called to meet in a hospital corridor outside Neil's room in the cancer hospital. Four doctors, a hospital chaplain and a hospital administrator stood with us, shaking hands, making small talk as they invited us into a room down the hall. When we entered the conference room, the chaplain, Father Holland said, "Mrs. Galloway, why don't you sit next to your husband? Heather, I'll sit next to you."

I said, "Please call us Marion and Dan. No need for formalities with us. We've been in and out of your hospital all year."

The rest of our family gathered around. Austin stood leaning against the wall. We were as crowded as packed sardines.

The meeting reminded me of one that could have

been held in Neil's small conference room in his downtown law office. Medical charts, also looking very legal, were there; lab reports and x-rays covered the table like trial exhibits. The only thing missing was our attorney, Neil.

In serious tones, Neil's primary cancer doctor bluntly said, "It's time to take Neil home and consider hospice care."

At that point, the conversation became a blur. In silence, I thought to myself, *what is the doctor saying? I am not ready to accept the words 'hospice care.'* Home care, maybe family care, seemed do-able. Never hospice care. Not for Neil. *I never really liked this doctor. We need another opinion.*

Dan questioned the fact that the hospital was ready to send Neil home. "Is there nothing else? Did his insurance stop paying? Why all of a sudden do you say there is nothing more to do and we must take him home? You think his days are numbered? Why now?"

The doctor said calmly, "It is time to come to closure. Your son is dying."

Inside my being, I screamed, *no. No. There is never closure and don't you dare tell me I am in denial.* **You** *are the quitters. We never quit. One of my son's mottos, since* *high school has been, 'never, never quit'.*

I took another of my frequent deep breath moments. I tried to rationalize any part of the conversation. *If Neil has to leave the hospital, it is God's way of telling us we can help heal him at home. I am not ready to give up. Neil is not ready to give up. I know my son. I will never be ready to give up. He will **never** be ready to give up.*

Why, then, did the doctors seem so certain? I tried not to panic.

Finally, the family came to the conclusion that Neil would go to our home. Going to his house would be too difficult for their children. Heather had her job and the children to care for. It was hard for her to agree but she knew it was best for her family. We hugged and cried and connected with a deep understanding. They said they'd come every day to visit Neil. By the time we walked out of the conference room, we each had our verbal hopes coupled with our unsaid, very real fears.

I wouldn't describe it as a good day.

* * *

I hadn't counted the times Neil traveled in an ambulance in the last year, but this time I wanted to believe it would be the last time he'd make that frightening trip. Not because he would die, but because we were on the way home for him to get well. The doctors had their chance, now we would find another way.

We were going home and he was going to recover.

I broke the rules and rode in the back of the ambulance with him. When the drivers told me I couldn't ride with Neil, I got nasty. Anger crept slowly and deliberately in my voice, "I go with my son or you won't get paid. I'll sign a waiver or whatever. I go or he stays here."

During the ride home, Neil's only words were, "Are you all right, Mom?"

"Of course. I'm thankful, Neil. We're going home to gather strength and get you well. We'll have a wonderful Thanksgiving and Christmas this year."

He gave me his sad but tough athletic smile. A chin up smile. He was tired.

We knew it would be better at our home. He had been raised there and it would be quiet. Heather, Patrick and Kellie could come and go and still have a sheltered place at their home, away from the fears we were all experiencing. Heather would know what to do and take the lead on all things involving the children. A hopeful situation, at last.

As soon as we knew he would be coming home, it took us less than twenty-four hours to transform our newly remodeled and enlarged breakfast room into a full-service hospital room. Three sides of his room were covered with glass windows that overlooked a lovely backyard waterfall.

Tall wind chimes hung on a Chinese tallow tree just above the waterfall. The chimes were very heavy and made a deep sound when there was a nice breeze. When caught by the wind, they played a low, rich melody and, with just a slight breeze, there was a note or two that resonated in a hauntingly beautiful deep and long-lasting *dong-dong-dong* . . . the pipes swayed and caught the vibrations. They made me think of the times Neil and I talked about bagpipes.

Wind pipes in our backyard. I'd not considered the similarity until now.

The chimes hung on a tree that was a Mother's Day gift from our sons in earlier years. A little tree was all they could afford. Considered a trash tree by most;

now, years later, we all loved it with its twisted trunk
and tall branches. We marveled at the height of the
tree on Neil's mid-October homecoming. It was taller
than the second story of our thirty-year-old home. The
tallow tree (they called it Mom's tree) gave forth a gift
of New England color in our Texas backyard. Reds,
gold, lime-green and dark maroon showed up for Neil.
Soon the patio would be covered with a patchwork
quilt of leaves. Never before had the colors been so
brilliant.

Beside his bed, we placed Neil's new electric
lounge chair. We had purchased the largest and most
comfortable chair we could find. When he complained
about the money we were spending, we told him to
consider the blue tufted chenille chair an early
Christmas gift.

He smiled again, retaining his sense of humor, and
said, "You know, you and Dad will travel 'round the
world on the frequent flyer miles you've gathered on
your credit cards, all because of my illness."

"Never, Neil, not unless you and your family go
with us."

We placed his tables and office supplies, his
bookcase and new portable radio with cassette and

CD player between his bed and chair. He called it a fine boom box. I'd not heard the term and was glad I picked one he liked.

Neil showed signs of energy as he helped arrange everything. He was glad to be home. The view from his newly equipped room was lovely. He spent his days looking out the floor-to-ceiling windows, watching birds and squirrels gather at the bird feeder. For most of his twenty-four hours, he listened either to music on his new boom box or replacing the music with audio motivational or religious tapes. At night, we left the outside lights on so he could see a family of raccoons when they visited the waterfall.

Neil had many recordings of his favorite performers. When he came home, we purchased some new ones. He especially enjoyed a CD, *The Chieftains Reel Music*. It was full of wonderful movie scores and lots of pipes and Scottish sounding music. The background music from *Treasure Island* brought to my mind the connections Neil felt to Scotland. Robert Louis Stevenson was from Scotland and also died at an early age. Stevenson was forty-two when his young and productive life ended.

Harold, our minister, came daily. Neil spoke to him

in private. When they'd finished, I'd walk Harold to his car, receiving my personal, spiritually uplifting lesson from our faithful friend.

And, much of the time, Neil continued to write on legal pads that he always kept within reach.

The first days he seemed to improve. He ate and walked out onto the patio and sat there for a while. We fixed a picnic table so that he was able to continue writing on his yellow legal pads. Several weeks passed and he talked less and less. He was a little more active but quiet.

Our discussions about dying stopped. His dad and I had a sense of his recovery. Neil did, too. Home-cooked meals and the parade of family and friends were akin to a vacation.

One day, after the house was quiet and we were alone, Neil began to talk with me again.

"You know, Mom, I appreciate you supporting me and my ideas. I know that sometimes my thoughts about building the bridge from eternity have sounded weird, but I hope you understand."

I did understand. His ideas were not so strange to me.

"Tell me a story, Mom. Your story."

With great hesitation, I pulled up a chair next to his and decided to tell him a part of my story.

"Okay, Neil, here's my secret. It isn't that you haven't recognized a great deal about your dad and me. You're the lawyer. You winnow out the truth and you do it well.

"If I were going to write this story, Neil, I'd call it, 'Love is the Link.'

"For years, I thought it strangely wonderful that books and music consumed so much of my life and thinking. Incredible things were revealed to me through books and music. I was afraid to tell others, for fear I might seem weird. I learned to accept this beautiful gift from God in secret.

"In my silence, my life and the lives of our family members were enriched because we shared the wonders of the written word and joys of music. Through the years, when there were problems, I prayerfully and secretly asked my Source to show us the way and to confirm if we were on the right paths for our solutions. I asked for answers and seemingly had them validated while I wandered through bookstores and listened to the music that followed me much of the time. I suppose you could call it a sort of prayer-like meditation.

"The answers came from deep in my being as I read the perfect passage from a book or heard the words of a song or melodies that assured me I'd made a connection to a universal creative force. The inspirational feelings came to me from my outer world but I think they were sent from another place. I kept to the belief that a rational person might see my acceptance of this inner sense as irrational. I felt I had to conduct myself, in every aspect of my life, in a manner the world saw as rational. Miracles happened in our family's lives and I remained silent because I was afraid. Why? I don't know."

"I knew it, Mom! You *do* understand what I want to do."

"Of course, Neil. I just don't want to think about any of it. I want you here with your wife, kids, and all of us. I want you well."

"Me. too. But I don't know if I can make it. I've been thinking since Harold came yesterday. He said some things that are still ringing in my head."

Our minister, Harold Kaiser, had been by our sides since the beginning of our ordeal.

I asked, "What did he say?"

"He quoted a passage from the Bible and said fear is

a difficult thing to overcome. He said I have my wonderful family and we will always be together in our spirits. He said we are not our bodies, we are *Spirit*. I remember one of the church speakers once said something like, 'we are not just our human bodies, we are spirits having a human experience.' Harold said life and death are each miracles. When we leave the bonds of this earth, it is like stepping into another room. You guys will still be here and I'll be in another room. Maybe we can't see each other or hear each other, but we will still know where we are. Do you think that, Mom?"

"I do, Neil. And more. I think we'll be forever linked by love. I guess that's why we're told God is Love. I think we're all connected together by those great, infinite and unending rooms of wisdom and knowledge. If we search and are led to be aware, and if we can sort through our feelings of lack, our God of love will help us find whatever we need, whenever we need it. I believe death is not what some think. It's good to think about it and I'm glad you and I share the beliefs that we can transcend and look to higher possibilities. We can talk about it whenever you want, Neil. This is a wonderful opportunity for us to learn and grow."

I was the one dying inside, but Neil seemed to be at peace on that day.

"Okay, now I know we are on the same page."

"Yes, we're on the same page, son. We are and will always be."

Neil smiled in a completely new way. He looked as I imagined he might look had he just won the biggest legal battle of his career. I could see his mind spinning, thinking. Planning.

"I'd like to take a nap now, Mom. I'm pooped out but when I wake up, I want you to be here. We need to talk."

After he woke, Neil planned his memorial service and took care of some legal matters. He requested the music be "Circle of Life," "Amazing Grace," and "A Mighty Fortress Is Our God." He requested that our minister tell Patrick and Kellie why their dad gave them *Lion King*™ stuffed animals for Christmas. He told me he'd promise not to die on Christmas Eve or Christmas Day. He wanted one more Christmas with the family.

Friends, legal associates, and family visited and things grew quiet and serious around our home.

Visitors spoke in whispers and rarely spoke directly to Neil. I hated that because I knew he could see his visitors and hear every word that was said. He wanted to communicate and tried by pointing over and over to a place above his feet, at the foot of his bed. The spot he wanted us to see, it seemed to me, became higher day by day; we wondered what he saw.

We never knew.

He squeezed our hands and looked at us with sad eyes. He held onto a little book and pointed to angels in the pictures. He hugged a huge, life-like, floppy, stuffed dog. Neil patted the dog on the head and stroked his soft furry back. I knew Neil was making a connection to the stuffed animal. We all wished his real dog, a beautiful snow white Samoyed called "Noel," was still alive.

It occurred to me that Neil might be pointing to an angel at the foot of his bed. Maybe like the one in his little book. I could imagine all day but we never knew.

He didn't talk again. Neil dropped into a world of music and dreams. Oh, we all talked to him. He just didn't respond any more. He was there for us but he wasn't talking anymore.

Then . . .

Parents *never* plan for things like those that
happened to us on New Year's Eve 1994, one week
after my Christmas Eve birthday when I had turned
sixty years old. Neil, our middle son, stopped
breathing. His good looks stilled; his blue eyes, bright
with intelligence and hope for the future, were closed.
His earthly songs were silenced. His books were
unfinished. He was only thirty-seven years old. The
doctors said he died of a rare type of brain cancer.
It doesn't matter what the age or how your son or
daughter dies, the hurt is the same. Conversely
nothing is the same. There is not a time when parents
want to accept the fact that their child is dying.
Some can never accept the death of their child.

There would be no closure for this mother.

I remembered his words, "We don't die. It can't
be that we die."

We added music Neil had not requested, a
recording of a bagpiper playing "Auld Lang Syne."
Every year, on December thirty-first, when we hear the
song of New Year's Eve written by Neil's favorite poet,
Robert Burns, I will forever wonder if Neil selected
this time to leave his earthly home . . . as the world
sings "Auld Lang Syne."

And, in our lives, it seems not a coincidence that the song is played by mournful sounds of bagpipes. I like to think that Neil is out there, on his bridge from eternity, looking forward to constructing future plans for the coming New Year towards us.

Searching for Impossibilities

If any of you lacks wisdom, ask God, who
gives to all generously and ungrudgingly,
and it will be given to you.

— James 1:5

INDUSTRIAL POLLUTION not often seen on the way to our ranch discolored the Gulf Coast prairie sky, and dust billowing from the dry gravel road dropped a fog-like cover on my white minivan, adding to a somber day in the country.

My heart and mind were debating back and forth. Neil had wanted me to enroll in novel writing classes at the university. It seemed very unreasonable and certainly out of character for me to follow his secret plans. He knew he was dying. There were no thoughts like his for me. I wouldn't let myself think such things. I knew he was a visionary kind of person; so at the time, his plan was one I decided to endure and try to play along and maybe understand.

Then, I told myself, there was no doubt about it. From time to time, I had begun to hear his "contact" songs on the radio, and they were played at just the times when I needed encouragement to live through my misery. I had the radio on where Neil decided it should be tuned. Even so, the songs could have been just coincidental. I could be making something out of nothing. But, then again, I needed something to get me through the days.

I tried to erase my thoughts and focus on the land our family knew and loved so well.

I drove past spindly patches of fragrant blooming trees. Native Texas huisache and mesquite, each prized as honey trees, dotted unimproved fields filled with various weeds. Misty, greenish-yellow pollens were blowing in the air. The trees and tall grasses swayed in the breezes that also caught seedpods as they dispersed their sticky spores. Dirt from the road and the floating seed mist lightly showered my van with a coating of allergens that made my eyes water and nose itch. Lately, no matter what the reason, they remained swollen and red.

Today, tears came easily as I thought of Neil and realized he wouldn't ride these roads this year, not ever again. On an earlier occasion, when I rode with him to the ranch, he'd driven his little Ford Ranger pickup. He'd laughed and hummed some of his favorite songs.

He'd quoted a new poem he'd written and talked about his writing class at the university. He shared an interesting legal case he'd recently acquired. He told me about a birthday celebration he and his wife were planning for their young daughter, Kellie. A wealth of memories rushed into my mind.

A deer jumped from behind a pile of brush by the side of the road, stopped for a second, turned his head to look at me and then retreated back to the fields. The buck startled me and I wished I could run away, too. Not even the lighthearted tune on the radio could lift my spirits.

My minivan, loaded to the gills, traveled a good bit more smoothly than it usually did because it was weighted down with heavy legal files from Neil's shuttered law office. His lawyer friends had advised that his files be kept for at least two years.

Tending to the closing of his practice had been my daily exercise for weeks, and the pain of his passing was ever constant as I carried out the necessary duties. His friends, colleagues, and our family offered to help move his files but it was a labor of love for me. It was something I wanted to do and something I'd told Neil

I would do. Even though the others didn't understand, I felt it was my task and, in truth, no one else had the time or the inclination to move more things from his office.

Since Neil's death I'd found I didn't talk much to anyone else but I talked to myself a lot. I talked to Neil, to God and to whatever else there was inside me. I was looking for a connection to our dead son, the secret link he said we would find to make us see meaning in this tragedy.

Questions, pleadings and sometimes a hint of an answer, all inside my head and heart, were now a part of my daily existence, and I realized I was on a constant lookout for the signs he said he would try to send if he didn't survive.

I kept asking myself, *where are the signs? What are they? How will I write the books he said he'd inspire in me? I'm afraid to try. And what about the music? Sometimes I hear one of the songs we discussed on the radio, but where are his beloved Scottish bagpipes? I remember the plans, but what if they don't work? What if there is no connection? Would I be better off never knowing? Am I just a deranged, grieving mother looking for messages from a son who is gone?*

I had to try to find the answers.

I waved and honked the horn as I passed the rustic, unpainted three-room house that belonged to our neighbors, the Richards family, who watched and tended our cattle each day. City folks need country folks to look after their places and we were glad we had worked out a mutually beneficial arrangement with our good neighbors.

Nettie Mae Richards stepped out onto her porch and waved back. I knew she wanted me to stop and visit, but I wasn't up to talking to her, not now. I promised myself I'd stop on my way back to Houston after I unloaded the van.

I managed to convince myself that storing Neil's files at the ranch, not keeping them in our garage in Houston, was a significant step toward letting go. I didn't want Nettie or anyone to stop this self-imposed ritual. There was a sense of uneasiness in the pit of my stomach and, as always since Neil's illness had begun eighteen months before, there was an aching in my chest.

I gulped hard as I took a long drink from the bottled water I carried in my cup holder. My mind sent me into a time warp as I thought of our family's original heritage in 17th century Scotland. The connection Neil felt to Scotland and Robert Burns, the Scottish poet, musician and songwriter, was uncanny. Throughout his college years, afterward and especially during the days of his illness, he remained fascinated with the lands of Rabbie Burns. He also loved the stories he'd heard and learned in the Texas Hill Country. Neil was himself a teller of tales, writer of poems, fantasy and history.

A beautiful red-tailed hawk swooped over my van and brought me back to the duty at hand. Again, I reminded myself that this trip and taking Neil's legal files out of Houston were important for my sanity.

If I am to continue to live, I must create some tiny space to begin healing the illness of loss that's consuming our family. My heart and mind repeated this conviction until it became as repetitious as a haunting melody.

At our vacant fishing cabin, everything I saw, everywhere I stepped reminded me of our family and of Neil. I felt as though a fog had descended. There was strangeness in the air, and I didn't feel open to opportunities or connections with our son. It occurred to me that I was taking part in a sad extended burial rite.

It took awhile to unload the boxes. I piled them in the abandoned cabin that showed the restoration attempts our family had made from time to time, in hopes of remedying the rotting condition of the structure.

On the nearby tributary to the lake behind the cabin, Neil had on several occasions spied an alligator. This morning, there were telltale signs of a trench where gators had slipped into the muddy, shallow part of the lake. I was on a gator lookout with every step.

I dodged a big beehive under the roof of the dilapidated porch. The bees came early each year, taking up residence among the rotting boards between the roof and the attic. It was sort of scary out there, alone. But I smiled as I remembered Neil's love for the place and the happiness he gained from fishing there. And, for a swift moment, I didn't feel alone. I needed more of those moments.

Whenever Neil had a few hours, he could be found fishing by the lake, on the lake or in the lake — whenever he took a notion to wade out before casting his hook. Neil loved fishing. He had planned to teach his young son all his favorite techniques. Neil's best friend, Matt Howard, had said at Neil's memorial service, "Some men live to fish. Neil fished to live! He understood the sport of fishing. He understood the fish."

It felt good to select this resting place for Neil's files. After all, they were his dead files. As far as I was concerned, the files were buried in the cabin on the ranch. DONE.

As I drove out the gravel road and past the barn, I had a strong feeling that I should drive back and see if everything was okay there. We'd built the barn as a family project and were proud it had weathered so well. No leaks and still a fine looking structure. I felt drawn to the barn.

The doors were heavy, and as I pushed, I realized it was the first time I'd been to the ranch alone. I wished for my husband, Dan, knowing he'd help push the doors open. I was sweating in the warm March humidity as I tried hard to move the doors.

Finally, I made a crack large enough to slip through. It was dim inside and I hoped some varmint wouldn't jump and run, knowing that's what I would do if anything jumped out at me.

As I moved farther inside the barn, I saw a school

desk with a stack of books piled on it. On top of the
books was a large varsity football helmet, the one that
had been custom-made for Neil, our "never, never
quit" football star.

I slowly walked to the helmet, picked it up and
dusted it off so the burnt gold and black Lion emblem
looked brighter. I held it close to my body and found
myself sobbing like I had never allowed myself to
cry before.

Music from *The Lion King*™ and sounds of the
bagpipes played at his memorial service flooded
my mind.

There was something about the moment beyond
words I could conjure. There were other things our
son had stacked around the barn, but I couldn't make
myself poke around for more. I had all I needed. I
wanted to get out of the barn and back on the road to
Houston. The helmet, an unexpected treasure, would
go home with me and, someday, I would show it to
his children and tell them stories about their dad's
football days.

As I was leaving the barn, I tried not to think about
Nettie waiting for me to stop and visit. It was too
coincidentally horrible that she and her husband had

recently lost their son, too. Victor, Jr. had died suddenly – a ruptured spleen, I think. But it doesn't matter how a child dies. The resulting loss is the same.

I remember that Dan would not, could not, go with me to visit the Richards family on the day of the funeral. Dan said it was work that kept him away. I knew better. Funerals will forever be hard for us. It took a lot out of me to go to Vic's funeral; but, in truth, it was best I went alone. The loss that my husband and I share is almost unbearable and somehow the grief seems ten times more difficult when we face it together.

Neil and Vic were the same age. Strangely, they were also the same age as Robert Burns when he died in Scotland. Three young men, thirty-seven years on this earth, each so different but connected by untimely and early deaths.

Neil and Vic knew one another in passing. They waved and honked horns and sometimes they stopped and talked about cattle or fishing. They were strong and carefree. They were good boys.

I knew I had to make myself stop and see Nettie. The house looked empty as I drove up into the dirt yard to the front porch. The dogs were resting under the house and didn't seem interested as I climbed the creaking steps. *Maybe she's not here.* When I knocked Nettie came to the lopsided screen door.

"How 'do, Mrs. G. We haven't seen much of you since. . . ." She looked down at the faded cotton slippers she wore on her swollen feet.

"How've you been?"

"Okay I guess, Nettie. I know it's been hard these last few months for you, too."

"Yes'm. Would you like to come in?"

She opened the screen door, and the dogs came up on the porch to try to get inside the little house.

"Shoo, you dogs, you git —"

Nettie pushed the dogs away and made a way for me to squeeze inside the door. As I stepped into the room and looked over Nettie's shoulder, I saw a framed photograph of Victor sitting on top of the TV. He was dressed in a football uniform. I looked again. He was holding his football helmet on his right hip.

I glanced back outside to the van where I knew Neil's helmet sat on the passenger side of the front seat. It was almost too much for me to cope with. I had a sense to turn and rush away, but I knew I had to stay.

"Nettie, I'm having a hard time making sense of

what has happened to us."

"Yes'm," she softly replied.

I didn't sit down. We stood uncomfortably. The tiny room was neat and dark. The single window had a shade pulled halfway down. The open door and the dim outside light from under the shade were the only sources of light.

Outside, a soft wind picked up and the screen door squeaked as it caught and moved in a cool breeze. The fogginess was gone. A late, much needed, afternoon shower seemed in the making.

We moved in unison as she opened the door and stepped outside on the porch again. Nettie looked off in the distance behind me towards the fields. Her gaze was fixed. As we struggled to hold on to our composure, our eyes were red-rimmed and sad, but we were not crying. We were trying to be strong for one another. I turned away and walked to the end of the porch, and she followed. We stood there and then, as if on cue, we looked at each other, reached out, and held tight for a brief moment. I felt a connection to her unlike any I had felt before. We knew each other's feelings and our hearts and spirits were seeking harmony.

As we stood there, a ray of light broke through the cloudy sky and shone on the field before us. A few seconds passed before I could make words come out of my mouth.

"Nettie, this is really beautiful. Have you ever seen sights like this out here?"

I was looking at the rainbow-like formation just at the top of where now three rays of light came down from the darkening clouds. The larger ray in the middle was bright, almost white, and so prominent that its bright shaft fell almost to the tops of the oak trees in the field. The two smaller rays had more color, not like the rainbow at the top of the cloud, but different because the sunlight on each side of the larger ray made the lesser lights glisten and seem to twinkle. We watched in silence.

"What are you thinking, Nettie?"

She didn't reply at first. Then, with her eyes showing great sadness, she said, "I think it's our boys tellin' us they's okay."

She paused and took a deep breath and whispered, *"I just wished we was, too."*

* * *

Going home, the van was lighter. It wasn't taking the gravel ridges well. It was empty. I wanted to be lighter too. I looked at the helmet and thought about the seventeen-year-old, 210-pound all-star center lineman who had worn it twenty years before.

Neil looks up into the football stands and sees his dad and me, the sun catching the gold outlined on his helmet. "Hi, Mom . . . hi, Dad. We can do it. Don't forget: never, never quit."

How many times had I heard Neil say, "We can do it, and never, never quit?"

Before this moment, I'd not let myself think seriously of the secret, detailed plans Neil made during the times we shared before his death. Since his death, nothing seemed possible anymore. I was to write his books for him and he was to be my spiritual inspiration. His after-death connections that might not happen were too difficult to consider. At least, that's what I thought until I saw the rays from the rainbow on Nettie's front porch. Could our newly planned journey have begun then?

I switched the radio to my easy listening station. I said, "If that was you, Neil, show me." I looked at the clock. It was 4:42 p.m.

There it was. Elton John's "The Circle of Life" . . . the song we played at Neil's funeral was now playing on my radio at the same time it had been sung at his service. I hadn't really expected to hear anything. It was enough to see the rays of light with Nettie. I was rattled and pulled the van off the road and listened to the words.

Maybe . . . the music could be a true gift from the other side of the bridge. It was one of the connection songs Neil planned for his experiment. I'll need to be open at all times. This is beyond serendipity. Neil, where are you?

After I listened to the radio, I pushed into the player the cassette of Kenny Loggins' new recording, the one Neil had in his player on the day he died. I listened intently to "The Rainbow Connection" and the complete album, as if hearing it for the first time.

Had Neil known what he was doing? It would be up to me to keep all my thoughts, my mind and heart open and wait for the signs.

Maybe we could write our books and he would send me the messages through music and bagpipes.

I asked myself questions I've repeated thousands of times since that day.

Is this possible? Is this rational? Rainbows as connections? Can the power of music unlock some of the mysteries from beyond? Could a spirit become a muse to an inexperienced writer? How are wonders of nature passed from the departed to the living?

As I traveled home to Houston and our grieving families, I wanted to try.

But would I? How could anyone survive this thing, the death of a child? My plan was to study hard and listen well. But, what was I doing? Was I losing touch with reality? *What is reality anyway? Dare I take the first steps? I don't know how to type, much less use a computer. I don't think I have the nerve to arrange my admission into the university and Neil's writing class.*

The Making of a Ghostwriter

Whatever you can do or dream you can do,
begin it. Boldness has genius,
power, and magic in it.

– Johann Wolfgang von Goethe

Level One Novel Writing

*I*T WAS 1995 AND A FEW months after Neil's death. Although it was his plan for me to continue his dreams of writing, I admit, on this day it seemed highly irrational. I seriously considered looking for a haven in a small cafe near the university and making it my headquarters for the next year. I was listening to 99.1, KODA, one of the planned stations. Neil wanted me to keep tuned on certain radio dials. There were no connection songs as I drove to the campus.

Before his death, Neil read Goethe to me from a book of quotations he had kept beside his bed in each of the many hospital rooms he'd occupied during the last year of his life. I had written the quote then, in one of the notebooks I kept in the book bag I carried when I stayed with Neil during his illness.

In preparation for my first day at the university, I searched for and found the quote at the top of one of my "hospital" notebooks I kept stored in my closet. I was looking for something of Neil's to take with me on my first day of class. I found his stacks of secret legal pads. I found my personal notebooks, too, but I knew I had to leave them all in the closet. He made me take an oath requiring me not to show his writings to others until after I completed the novel writing course and had finished "our" novel about building his bridge.

Finding nothing more I wanted to take, Goethe's words accompanied me to my new novel writing class. I penciled the words at the top of an empty notebook assured that Neil would like my choice.

As apprehensive as I was, I had no idea what it would mean to be a member of the class or how much I'd need to fake it. My palms were sweaty and I knew I looked pale. I'd no typing skills and had never touched a computer. I had only my fresh spiral notebook, a pen, and a pencil. More than fifty years before, I had the same supplies as I began my only semester of college in the small junior college near my hometown of Ida, Texas. I don't remember being frightened as a young woman back then, but I was frightened now on this return trip to higher education.

I swallowed my fears. I knew there would be no hiding in the small cafe near campus. I had to make the effort. I was on my way to my son's planned adventure.

I was early. Too early. I decided to find the classroom and settle into a desk the farthest distance from the front of the room, and nearest the door, so I would have a clear path of escape. I watched as the students began filling the room. Students confident of themselves and the situation had no qualms about taking seats in the front, but the back of the room also filled. The latecomers were in the middle. Soon, Level One Novel Writing overflowed into the hall and upper-level student teaching attendants scurried to find extra desks and chairs.

His name was carefully printed on the blackboard. It was a name that I couldn't pronounce. I wrote it down and wondered how on earth any Texan could pronounce his name. I hoped he would tell us he had a nickname or something other than the name on the blackboard. I wondered about his country of origin.

At the appointed time, the professor rushed in,

passing right by my desk. I was immediately scared to death. I had no idea the teacher would look like he did. Neil hadn't warned me. He had said only that he was a great teacher. Maybe I enrolled with the wrong instructor. The man who passed my desk did not strike me as a man who would inspire or impress Neil.

He had full, dark hair that flipped up on one side, almost covering his eye on the other. It hung to his collar, making his already dark skin and eyes look darker, and the circles under his eyes more pronounced. He wore a loose fitting white coat, baggy off-colored pants tinged yellow, and a purple shirt with an outlandishly bold and colorful tie. He tossed several tote bags on his desk and immediately began handing out notebooks. He said, "My name is on the blackboard. You will call me Professor." I heard his words about his name and I heard, "Call me Professor," after that, I had no idea what he was saying. He spoke with an East Indian accent and he spoke at first too slow, then too fast. Too loud and then too low. Could the others understand him? Still talking, he began to hand out what seemed to me to be a test.

That's it. I can't stay here another minute. I must be in the wrong classroom. Neil can't help me here. How can there be a moment of peace or time for inspiration around this pompous, stalking, impossible young man? I am in the wrong classroom.

The Professor said, "Fill in your answers to these questions and hand them back to me before you leave." The bald man in front of me began to blush red at the neck of his T-shirt and the redness followed a path all the way up to the top of his head.

I sensed fear all around me.

The Professor began speaking and I took notes. I strained to hear and understand him. He said, "You will study a complex art form. If you want to write a novel, you will take five to seven years. You will write until complete."

Do I have seven years left to live? Who knows? But surely, I can do it more quickly than that!

At the break, I stayed at my desk. I looked at the questions on the test form. "Who is your favorite author and why?" My mind went blank. Our walls at home are full of books. I couldn't remember an author. Who was Neil's favorite? Who's mine? How do you spell Crieghton . . . Michael Crichton? No, I've never read him. How about the man who won the Pulitzer? Yes, I'll say him. Everyone is talking about his book.

How do you spell McMurtrey (McMurtry)? Larry who?
If I misspell the author's name, the Professor will know
I haven't actually read my "favorite" book. Who wrote
Moby Dick?

I am going to leave now. This is not the place for me. I
am stupid. I am crazy. I'll find that cafe and spend the year
depending on Neil's spirit to be my teacher. It will be our
secret. It will be easier than this. I'll leave this classroom
and never come back!

While the break was still going on, I rushed to my
car and got in. I was trembling. I turned on the radio
but there was nothing. No messages from beyond. I
glanced at the Professor's bound colloquium and
opened to read the first pages. Cold chills went up my
spine. The Table of Contents was all I needed to see.
The Professor was teaching "Foundation Courses."
Level Two was called, "The Bridge."

I gathered my notebooks and walked hesitantly
back to the classroom. The Professor looked at me
uncomprehendingly. He didn't know who I was – or
that I was back and would stay, at least through Level
Two of his novel-writing class.

This impossible man is going to teach me how to build a
bridge, so I'll listen to him. No matter that he doesn't know

the bridge is to be from eternity back to me. Maybe the Professor's message will be Goethe's message. If I begin, boldly, there will be "genius, power and magic in it." Will he be our writing contact? Is it worth two college semesters? Seven years to write a book, indeed!

* * *

The next few weeks attending the university taught me a big lesson. I was in deep trouble, way over my head. The Professor was difficult. Difficult in many ways. I couldn't understand half his words. I asked and he gave me permission to tape record his lectures. One try at recording a lecture told me I'd be better off learning to understand him. I tried to adjust to his accent and the tones of his voice. He spoke like rapid gunfire. He was an excitable man. He loved his work. He had favorite students and I was not one of them.

He insisted every written assignment be identical in form. I needed a computer. It was necessary for his class. I attended every session even though I missed handing in the first three assignments. Denial again.

I could tell the Professor was ready to kick me out of class but I didn't want to believe it.

Then, at break during my third class, he called me outside the room and into the hall.

"Ma-ri-on, what is the matter with you? Do you wish to continue?"

I lied. "My computer is broken. I'm waiting for it to be fixed."

Then I added, "Yes, I do want to continue. Very much. I've read all the assigned readings and have the written assignments in my notebook. Could I turn those in today or read them in class?"

He looked astounded. He seemed frustrated and then, quizzical. I didn't duck my head. I held it high. I wanted to show strength to this man, this mystical engineer with an English degree who knew not what he was doing for me. I needed him to help build our bridge. Neil's and mine.

"Ma-ri-on, go to the library and complete your assignments on the computer. You must complete according to the instructions written in the booklet you received on the first day. Do you understand? You must follow the rules before re-entering the classroom. You are excused from class today. Pick up your belongings and when you return, it must be with your assignments, following all the rules. Go now to a computer on campus."

He turned, flipped his mop of black hair away from his face, and calmly strode back into an already-dwindling classroom.

I went back into the room, picked up my tote bag and left. I could feel the group looking at me and knew they were wondering if the Professor had excused another person from his class. When others left after a hallway lecture with the Professor, it seemed a sure-fire force out. Maybe the class thought they wouldn't see me again. I walked steady and made not a hint of an expression while the remaining men and women tried not to stare. They would see me again. I would figure out a way.

Upset, and trying to get a grip on the situation, I decided to walk around the university campus. I needed to calm myself and make plans to re-enter Level One Novel Writing. I was so nervous before my first class, I hadn't noticed how startlingly beautiful the campus was. The handsome buildings with long arched porticos fronted by green lawns and shaded by stately but gnarled, old trees spoke to me. I sat on a bench beneath a huge oak. A small town girl from Ida, Texas, I had no expectations of ever sitting on a bench at this well-known campus asking myself,

"What do I do next?"

Had Neil stepped outside and rested on this bench during his class break? I looked for a connection. I took a deep breath and wondered if I could carry out this crazy plan. It was depressing. *Yet, I need to be open and find a sign. Follow Neil's rules, not the Professor's.* I could have more than one set of rules to follow in this engineering feat.

Then, admiring the porticos, I imagined the arched brick columns to be like the underside of a bridge. *Yes, that's where I am. I am in deep water under the university bridge.*

I needed another scheme to follow for a short period. Slowly, the answer came.

I admit there were problems to face. I would be determined. I would not drop out. I would do what ever I must do. I must remember, "Never, never quit."

First things first. I didn't know how to work my new computer. My entry-level computer class was three weeks away. I needed to learn now. But what to do to get back into class?

I know. I'll go to the office supply store and try to hire someone who will put all my assignments in a computer program, follow the instructions to a tee. Make them perfect and return to the next class. Assignments in hand. I can do it. I must. I'll show him.

Still scheming, I thought:

I know I can gain his sympathy if I tell him I am Neil's mother. However, the plan Neil contrived won't allow me to tell the Professor why I am there. Not until the book is complete. The Professor has no clue. I have to take precautions to follow Neil's plan.

I told myself there is no way I could be mistaken for Neil's relative. Among other things, I thought I might look too young. After all, I married at seventeen, near my eighteenth birthday. We had Neil two and a half years later. He was sandwiched between his two brothers. He was the ever-present filler in the middle, making their little boy unit complete. First Travis, then Neil, followed by Austin. Our family was complete by the time I was twenty-one.

To help things along in my quest for youth, I had colored my hair for the first time in my life. There was no gray. And I'd lost weight.

When I made application to the university, I wrote

my maiden name using a hyphen along with Galloway. It looked different. I hoped it would look like a bestselling writer's pen name. I used three names: Marion Maureen Dunlop-Galloway. No member of my family knew I'd use three names for my new life. I thought my classmates and the Professor saw me as a strange bird. What a splendid hoot. Neil must have loved it.

* * *

Folks were beginning to wonder why I'd isolated myself and hadn't asked others for help. I wished I could have shown them that our family was totally stricken with grief. No one could begin to understand what I was doing. Everyone thought I was under-reacting to Neil's death. Each family member was doing the best they could. The idea that I would try to further my education at a time like this was inconceivable to my family and friends. And I tried my best to show I was in complete control. I tell you this—it was not me in that classroom. It was not a student. It was a driven mother reaching for an impossible solution. I avoided contact with the students. I tried to avoid contact with the Professor. It was like a dream.

A place I was and was not.

Never, Never Quit

No one knows what he is able to do until he tries.

Pubilius Syrus (circa 50 BC)

A month later, I'd muddled through a weekend computer class. Two weeks after the computer class, I found myself in the hall of the university again. Another after-class meeting requested by the Professor.

"Ma-ri-on . . . what is it you find so difficult about following the format for your assignments? If I tell a student to follow the rules, I expect the rules to be followed."

He pronounced each word with a distinguished flair and placed accents on the wrong syllables of my name. He opened his loose-fitting jacket and adjusted his shoulder pads as he spoke his admonition. He tightened his tie, just a bit. The Professor was full of enigmas: I could see a touch of Mahatma Gandhi (with a full head of hair) and when the professor wore his straw hat, a bit of W.C. Fields. He was almost never still. He was pacing, marking papers while we read, and shaking the hair off his forehead. If not moving, one might expect he was thinking about moving. He would make a nice whirling dervish.

* * *

I didn't have the nerve to confess my failure in computer class. I'd learned to start the thing, use the printer and got into the swing of my self -taught hunt and peck system on the keyboard. That's all I could take in. It was a waste of good money. The instructions were like another foreign language. I couldn't follow instructions in my novel writing class without learning the computer and even though I gave it a good try, I had decided I was computer-dyslexic and certainly illiterate with a host of newfound learning disabilities both with the computer and in the Professor's novel-writing course.

I couldn't stand the thought of failing Level One. I felt haunted. I was driven to carry on and, at the same time, I was feeling guilty because I'd been bluffing. I remembered one of our family motivational mottos, "You must be willing to do whatever it takes."

I hadn't considered the "lesson" we taught our sons might have meant lying. Not under any conditions. Maybe I needed forgiveness.

* * *

The Professor stopped me in the hallway again. "Ma-ri-on, we must schedule a meeting. Perhaps after class on Saturday. If you do not wish to continue, I'd like to know the reason. If you need help, I will find someone to help you."

"Professor, please have patience with me. I'm mentally slow, it's a disability." I lied to him for the second time.

Did he know when someone was lying? It seemed as if he thought I was hiding something. Was my guilt showing through?

"I've handled this problem for years and I'll handle it again. Please give me a little more time. I'll learn the computer soon."

"Ma-ri-on, you should tell the university such

things before you begin classes. Your teacher wants to know if you have learning difficulty."

"Please, Professor. I can do this class. I'll do whatever it takes."

"Very well, Ma-ri-on, let's see what we can do. We will meet at 2:30 pm in Room 212 next Saturday afternoon."

"Yes, sir. I'll be there." I resumed my newly acquired brave stance and was ready to be excused from class again.

He nodded and turned abruptly and headed back to the classroom and I headed toward the front door. He stopped and turned my way,

"Ma-ri-on, follow me into the classroom. You are not dismissed. I will tell the students you are not familiar with your new computer program. I must tell them you have two weeks to have your papers in the proper order according to the rules of this class. It is time I remind the class the importance of correct procedures when handing in the assignments. Writers must be disciplined and professional at all times. There can be no excuses if one expects to become a novelist. Level One is to determine if there are any writers among us."

No! He's going to make an example of me. I am going to excuse myself from class. Neil, you trickster, how could you expect me to work with this man?

Still in the hallway, in a whisper, he said,

"Ma-ri-on, I expect you to show me you are a writer. I expect you to show what can happen when one has a desire to write. I think you have the desire. Do not disappoint your teacher."

I had one week to improve.

*   *   *

I forced myself to keep trying. "Whatever it takes," I kept saying to myself while reminding Neil's spirit I was begrudgingly giving it my best.

I purchased books for beginners and for students in the lowest grades. I visited a large computer store, found a word processing program for beginners, one for students in grades five through twelve. The program seemed easy and I felt I could progress to the high-school level with practice. I learned to do my version of "cut and paste." I typed the numbers of the pages on a piece of paper, cut them out, and pasted them in the correct places on my assignments. I typed a perfect heading with all the information required by the professor on another piece of paper. I cut out the heading information and pasted it on each assignment with clear tape. I had to type different dates on paper so I could cut and paste the appropriate dates on each assignment. All done, I drove to the copy store and made the twenty-five copies required before entering the classroom. I gave new meaning to "cut and paste."

Unfortunately, the Professor noticed the difference when I began to write with my computer. My papers looked as if a fifth grader had prepared them. I still didn't know how to find the correct fonts. Always, I made excuses for myself.

Our completed works were placed on the Professor's desk at the beginning of each session. He checked carefully to see if he'd received the three assignments required by each student. If the assignments were not in complete adherence with his rules, those papers were put at the end of three stacks in front of him. Mine, with his quick glance in my direction, were always placed on the bottom. The fifth grade level computer program was not working. I read my work to the class, last. Every time.

I knew I had to learn quickly. I prayed for guidance.

I lacked courage. I kept looking for encouragement.
I listened to the radio and looked for signs of Neil.
There was nothing notable anywhere. I wondered if
the plan would actually lead me anyplace other than
to a psychiatrist. The Professor was frightening. When
he looked at me, he peered. It didn't feel normal.

There was one good thing: he seemed interested in
my bogus learning disabilities. He gave a short lecture
on an essay a student in another class was writing
about overcoming dyslexia. He knew I knew he was
talking to me. He peered directly at me during most
of his lecture.

I asked myself, *is all of life about overcoming? What
am I doing here? As if there was not enough to learn,
now I am making this man question if I am able to learn.*

I would need to progress past fifth grade computer
level in a week.

* * *

By the time the Professor and I met for our
conference, I was uncertain if I could continue to fake
my way. My cut and paste system was working on a
higher grade level and I had another computer class

scheduled. However, my papers were still on the bottom of the stack. I'd come to the conclusion I needed to get past Level Two. I was halfway through Level One. Still, nothing made me think I could become a writer. My teacher seemed aloof and I felt a buffoon in class.

* * *

I walked into Room 212 and found him sitting at a long table with a large pile of papers in front of him. He was reading and correcting student assignments. He stood up and motioned for me to sit across from him. I was surprised when he stood up. I was nervous. He seemed at ease. He wore another loose outfit, this time a gray Nehru shirt with matching pants, the shirt had full sleeves. His attire made him look more an East Indian stranger and less my teacher. On the table, there were his ever-present tote bags full of papers and books.

The Professor began,

"Ah yes, Ma-ri-on, we must have this talk if you wish to continue. We must see what we have to do here. There are important things for us to know. We are stressing your lack of computer knowledge too much. It is true you must adhere to the rules and you will need to continue to study your computer training. But we must remember, above all, that a writer works with word pictures, not a computer. Pictorials. Dynamic adventure. If you worry about the computer so much, you will have no time to think of the words.

"Showing your story is the important thing. You must never tell me your story. I do not wish to be *told* anything. You will paint word pictures for me to visualize. If you are a writer, you will wish to share your words with the world and make them memorable. Mine is not a class to teach you to live your life. It is for you to show me a story with characters and emotion. It can be your story but you paint the pictures. It is fine if you wish to tell others about yourself. I don't wish to be told. If telling is important to you, you do not belong in my class. To become a writer, we must not be self-absorbed persons who keep words of worth to ourselves."

He got up and walked to an open zippered bag, and searched around for a bottle of medication. Aspirin, I thought. I could have used a couple, too. He walked outside the room, leaned over the water cooler and took whatever it was. He came back and said,

"Ma-ri-on, what is your problem? You are too serious. If you find my studies too difficult, you should be about your work elsewhere."

I was dumbfounded. He was on to me. I thought I was going to cry. Was he trying to force me out of his class? I felt my face turning red and my hands were wet. I couldn't tell him why I was there. He'd think I was lying again, for sure.

Then, the Professor shocked me. He gently said,

"Ma-ri-on, your papers are good. I don't know where you are headed with your writing. I am interested. I like you. You may continue the class. Nonetheless, we must follow the rules. We have this meeting so we will know what is most important. Our words."

He shifted in his chair and looked straight at me.

"To be admitted to the Level Two writing class, you must submit an Application to Proceed and an original writing that shows me that you have mastered the requirements of Level One. Begin working on it now. If you do not write a good application, you will not proceed to Level Two. You have much to learn. I think you will become a writer, Ma-ri-on."

At first I was speechless. I managed to mutter, "Yes sir, thank you, Professor."

Remembering what I had to do, I spoke in a more confident voice, "I'll do better, and I promise I'll work harder. I have a goal, Professor. I must become a writer. I need you to help me. Please."

We smiled at one another. He reached across the table and almost took my hand but he held his up and drew it back. For the first time, I hoped we might have a chance of becoming friends. He looked so young but there were airs of an ageless man around him. I wondered if, under the cover of his exterior showmanship, I could find the wise teacher, the unusual man Neil had liked so well.

Neil had seen something in him and had sent me to him. I needed to continue, as long as he'd have me in his class. I'd forget about what I lacked. I'd stop fighting the lessons in learning, the lying, and feeling sorry for myself. I'd let this man teach me. I had to do it for Neil.

Leaving room 212, I walked out on to the campus. I was deep in thought when a strong wind sweeping across the campus parking lot surprised me. The sky was clear and the sun was shining. I reached up to

smooth my ruffled hair and caught a glimpse of a white
seagull flying high, circling with the wind. The
university, located miles from the Gulf Coast, had
many doves and pigeons around the stately buildings
but a seagull was out of place.

Thoughts came swirling inside my head. I
remembered the words,

"You'll need to be open and look for me, Mom.
Unexpectedly, there may be something to remind you
I am there."

Neil had said, "Here, take my cassette albums and
listen to them. Don't forget *Jonathan Livingston
Seagull*."

But I had forgotten. I couldn't remember the story.
Where was my memory? I wanted to stay and watch
the seagull longer. I strolled off the parking lot towards
the lush green grass and trees on campus. A large
ornamental rock was nearby. It was a perfect resting
place. My head remained tilted with my eyes trained
upon the sky. I searched for the story of Jonathan. Was
he there, flying high, or was the scene in my mind?

Yes, the seagull was there, by himself, climbing and
circling. Diving low then all at once climbing to reach
a height so high he vanished from my sight. I sat there

for a few minutes. The gull came again, this time diving to the edge of the trees, looping around, and then soaring upwards again. And he was gone. Vanished. I wanted to rush home and find the cassette album and the book. Was it possible Neil had sent me a lesson, a book or a cassette album that might relate to the Professor and my class? A message from *Jonathan Livingston Seagull*?

Across the parking lot, I saw the Professor looking at me as he walked to his car. I thought he might come my way so we could talk more but he didn't. Maybe later, I thought. We each had places to go and things to do.

I would begin to write my Application to Proceed. And listen to the cassette about Jonathan and remember what Neil had planned for me. I was excited about seeing the seagull, or was it Jonathan or Neil? I considered it to be a message from above. I knew I had to search for answers and get through my fears. The sighting of the seagull at that time and place was important to my future. My life was changing, just as Neil's changed when he found his high school football and college plans would need to change because of a serious head injury. He didn't give up then. Neil didn't give up later when he was planning his miraculous bridge. The Professor was right. I had much to learn. I would not give up.

* * *

Richard Bach wrote *Jonathan Livingston Seagull* in 1970. It was the year Neil was injured in a high school football game and briefly knocked unconscious. Although he continued to play in the game and attended school for several days, he complained of headaches and stopped eating. We took him out of school and for a week searched with the doctors for a reason. Finally, his team doctor referred him to a well-known diagnostic group of medical doctors. They discovered he'd developed a subdural hematoma, a blood clot in his head.

Neurosurgeons were consulted and as soon as his problem was confirmed, he was rushed to surgery to drain the clot in his brain and save his young life. It was a big thing in his high school and a frightening experience for our family. He was a star player and a leader in his class. For days while he was in the hospital, his doctors, friends, coaches, our ever-present minister and our family kept vigil. Thinking back, I remembered how many friends and family members were always there for him.

The injury changed his life. Among other things, Dan and I were very happy he would never play football again. Several university football coaches were looking at him and he was not yet a senior. The coaches said Neil had all the attributes necessary to receive a university scholarship. Neil had been working hard to play football at a top-flight university.

I was working at a neighborhood bookstore when Neil was hurt. *Jonathan Livingston Seagull* was one of those tiny little books that caught on like wildfire and became a best seller. I purchased it for Neil and he read it while recuperating from his surgery. He enjoyed the book and recommended it to the doctors and nurses and everyone who came to visit. I heard him when he told his favorite doctor friend, an orthopedist, "Doctor Jay, why don't you read this book? It's by Richard Bach. It's like a fable about a seagull that wants to be the greatest flyer of all time. But I think the book is about feats of courage and self-sacrifice.

This bird, Jonathan, was dismissed from his flock and found he had the time to more fully develop his skills to become a better gull. In doing so he reached higher levels of achievement."

Neil continued, "I think my injury may have taught me to reach higher than a football scholarship. I am curious about my life path now. Maybe there are more important things for me to do."

His friend, Dr. Jay, said, "You are very probably right, Neil."

Yes. I think I saw Jonathan. And I felt Neil was flying higher now. Far higher than any of us ever thought he would.

Thinking back, maybe it was, in part, books that changed Neil's life and not so much the injury. He became more reflective and wrote poetry. He read the poets, with special focus on Robert Burns, Walt Whitman, Robert Louis Stevenson and W.B. Yeats. He read the Bible, the Transcendentalists and especially enjoyed every fantasy book by Terry Brooks. He revisited a favorite group of books by C.S Lewis, *The Chronicles of Narnia*. Neil found inspiration in *The Lion, Witch, and the Wardrobe*. Lewis' lion, Aslan, began Neil's interest in mythical lions. Neil told me he considered Aslan to be a spiritual lion. It was interesting that his football team was called "Lions." No wonder and I supposed, it was not an accident, that in his last year of life Neil connected to the Disney movie, *The Lion King*™ and its spectacular music.

There was little doubt in my mind. The seagull I saw on campus was a reminder that Neil was watching over me in class. On that day, I felt he was with me. After all, Neil said he would be my Muse. I felt I had my message and I hoped I could write, as Richard Bach had done, what I visualized in my heart. I had my doubts, I was no Bach. I had no illusions of becoming a great writer like Richard Bach.

*   *   *

The Professor made it clear that every student needed to write a convincing Application to Proceed to the next level of his class. Level One was almost over and I was spending all my free time trying to come up with an original paper to submit to him. I had Neil's notebooks, and his writings he hadn't wanted to talk about. Maybe I could find one or two of his Applications to Proceed and find an idea telling me what I might write.

I went to the locked closet and gathered a stack of his legal note pads and began to look through each one. Poetry, lots of poetry but no Applications to Proceed. When I'd searched five or six legal tablets, I came across notes he'd written for an outline for one of his Applications to Proceed. Neil hadn't finished the Application because he became ill. I figured if he'd planned to be my Muse, I could use the outline and we could write it together. It would be my first attempt. He'd made plans to visit a bookstore and write about his experiences there. It seemed a fine focus for my Application. I wouldn't be using his words, only his notes to lead my way. I felt it was an important find. I'd come back to the poetry soon.

Before following Neil's outline, first I sat at my computer and wrote the prerequisites for Level Two. I prepared a folder containing my completed assignments from Level One. If I could convince the Professor I had a reason to continue and passed his test with improved writing skills, he would admit me to the next level. I wondered how many in Level One would make Level Two. I'd seen, first hand, that he was a demanding teacher. I was ready to proceed if he'd have me.

* * *

The Application to Proceed was inspired from the notes of my Muse. I could almost hear Neil saying, "Tell the Professor what you and I have discussed. But don't mention me, not yet."

Marion Maureen Dunlop-Galloway
3122 Billenbrook Lane
Warm Springs, Texas 97804
Application to Proceed to Level Two
April 8, 1996

Who's Afraid of the Big Bad Wolf?

I am reminded of a children's bedtime story as I write my first Application to Proceed into the next phase of my Novel Writing class. It's the story of the three little pigs. In earlier years, I read the story to our three sons, many times. I remember discussing with the boys what I thought was the meaning of the story. At risk of sounding too much the mother and not enough the writer, I'd like to show the comparison between the little pigs and myself.

The three little pigs were building their homes. The first two little pigs didn't prepare for possible problems in the overall strength of framing their structure and didn't make solid foundations as they built their new homes. Because their homes were weak, the first two little pigs underestimated the Big Bad Wolf when he knocked on their doors and "huffed and puffed" until he ultimately destroyed the pigs and their homes.

The third little pig, taking a lesson from his brothers and seeing the disasters that can happen when not prepared, took great care in building his home – building a strong foundation and working very hard on the overall structure. Because the third little pig used his awareness and planned for his future, the house the third little pig built withstood

I

the attack of the Big Bad Wolf. The moral stands clear:

It is best to begin with plans for good structure and strong foundations if we expect to go forward in any endeavor.

There have been times during the last few years when I've felt the attack of the Big Bad Wolf close at hand. Had it not been for a knowing within me and the recent stability of the Novel Writing classes with the Professor at the helm, I might have followed the path of the first two little pigs.

Since signing up for the Novel Writing class, I've spent a good bit of time reassessing, rethinking, and reviewing the book I am beginning in Level One Novel Writing. From the beginning, I have pushed very hard to keep myself on track with the class and especially with the story. I have wandered and floundered all around the paths that would lead me back to my true desire for my novel. For a time, I felt hopelessly lost and wasn't willing to look for an answer.

It has been the reassessment of my desire to take this class and to learn to write that have led me to confront issues and questions I must face before advancing. I must think about my honesty in the classroom and in my writing. Writing for me, in this class, is risky business. Am I willing to show my story to the world?

Telling the story isn't enough. I know I must be willing to do whatever it takes to show my love for this story, even though I am in emotional pain some of the time. Am I willing to show the world I have been in pain? In the good

II

times, will I be enthusiastic? How could I not be with the Professor at the helm? Will I be able to find a balance in my novel?

I love the questions that come to mind during this reassessment; however, at times I hate to face the questions. Back and forth, in writing and in life, always searching for answers. Nothing unique about that.

What may be unique and what I risk in writing is the way I find many answers. Maybe I can best explain like this.

A few weeks ago, I found myself down-spirited and sad, doubting if I could continue my writing and if I was doing the "right thing" in staying in the class that is beginning to mean so much to me.

Up front, I am going to tell you that whenever I have questions of this magnitude, I go to a Source that may seem unusual to the outside observer. I look for meaning, for answers to the questions and for words that will show me I am on the right track in my thinking. I have done this kind of searching since I was a small girl. I think many people do the same kind of searching on some level. What may be unusual about me is I find my Source is available through books and music.

For years, I thought it strange that books and music consumed so much of my life and thinking, so strange that I was afraid to tell anyone the uniquely wonderful things that were revealed to me through books and music. In my silence, my life and the lives of our family members, particularly our three sons, have been enriched because we shared the rational wonders of the written word and joys of music. When there were problems, I prayerfully asked my Source to show us the way and to confirm we were on the right paths for our solutions as I made my connections and had them validated while I wandered through bookstores and listened to the music that seemed to follow me much of the time. Miracles happened in my life and I remained silent because I was afraid. Why? I don't know. What I do know is I found comfort in looking, but never expecting.

Last Sunday, I visited the crowded Half-Price Bookstore on Belvedere St. Its slightly disorganized appearance with the many tables stacked with books and more books stuffed in every nook and cranny brought an awesome sense of quietness to my searching self.

I asked myself, "what will make it right to tell the truth, in my novel, about the mystical connections and inspiration between family members, living and dead?" As soon as I walked inside the store, I felt directed to a table in the back. The first book I picked up was a well-worn paperback. The author . . . Michael Crichton. I hesitated because I remembered Crichton was an author I'd never read. I smiled because, up to that point, I'd always thought he was "too scary." I put the book down . . . just another scary book. But then, I thought *I am here for answers and maybe I should have another look.* The first chapters: "Medical Days," "Cadaver."

No, no this is not for me.

I put the book down and began to walk away. But then I

went back and looked at the cover of the book. Dare I look further?

The title: *Travels.* Written in 1988. The cover blurbs: "the real story of a writer's search for the wonders of the world – and for his true self" . . . "just the ticket for those who would escape, for once, to themselves – and perhaps know risk for the first time" . . . "a quest across the familiar frontiers of the outer world, a determined odyssey into the unfathomable, spiritual depths of the inner world" . . . "disturbing, curious, sensible and irreverent."

Is there an answer here?

As I pondered on the used paperback, the background music began playing Elton John's "Circle of Life" from the Disney movie, *The Lion King.* The song "Circle of Life" is more than important to our family.

Shaken but certain, I purchased the paperback book, *Travels.* . . . The price, $1.98.

I drove home wondering if the words of the book would be as profound as was the moment of discovery. They were. I had my answers – my validation – certainly my connections to enter the next level in writing, in which I will learn to write about building a bridge between time and space. There is no doubt in my mind that I am to continue to write, and I am to continue to try to write my novel so it might be read by readers who have a spark for "the irrational, the curious and the sensible." I can mix and match. There are fears, of course, but it can be done. I will need help. Especially, I need the help of my fellow students

V

and my newfound teacher.

Like the third little pig, I will need to build a strong foundation and structure. I feel blessed because I have been a part of the process from Level One. It is in our continued growing and exploring that we learn what it takes to become a writer.

Who's afraid of the Big Bad Wolf? Am I afraid? Yes. But I'm prepared to work and build to survive.

The Application changed a good bit as I wrote it. I used Neil's notes on Crichton, and the idea of the three little pigs. My first completed Application to Proceed was, in a way, our first go at Ghostwriter and Muse. My written words were simple. Neil wouldn't have written so simply. He would have been more detailed and used a more legalistic style. But, with his ideas, I hoped it would pass the scrutiny of our Professor.

* * *

Looking back, I think the following days may have contained a few miracles, of sorts. If not miraculous, the events seemed unbelievable to me. A folder containing all of our assignments from Level One along with our Application to Proceed were required to be placed in a packet addressed to the Professor. We were instructed to place a self-addressed, stamped envelope inside our packet so he could return his comments and hopefully, assignments for Level Two. I followed every detailed step written in the book he gave us at the beginning of Level One. I waited for the return of my self-addressed, stamped envelope.

I walked to the mailbox every day. I used the time to consider what I might do if I didn't make the next level. On a few days, I began my walk talking to Neil. Apologizing for not making the class, if I didn't.

"Fear is a worrisome thing," I said to Neil. "You are sure and strong. You knew I'd need the Professor to complete your plans. I don't want to let you down, son. I just don't have the training to do this. If the Professor kicks me out, I don't know what I'll do."

About that time, I looked up and saw Jonathan, our seagull. He was flying high and swooping down and around. I smiled. That seagull had a way of being where he was meant to be. *Maybe my imagination again.* Nonetheless, he was there. I began humming, "Circle of Life," from *The Lion King*. As I sought to remember each of the song's words, I made my way to the mailbox.

I was pleased when my packet arrived, much earlier than I'd expected. I was afraid to open it. I walked home so I could sit down and pour a glass of iced tea. I knew it is normal to tear open an important package, getting the news as soon as possible. I couldn't find the nerve. I had a brief thought that I should bypass Neil and go straight to God to plead my case. I was afraid, again. My heart was pounding. I drank my tea and carefully opened the package with a kitchen knife.

Inside the envelope, along with my returned assignments, I found another envelope. It was written on letterhead from the Novel Writing course at the university. I opened the envelope and read a letter from the Professor. He had sent a typed schedule of the times, dates and locations of Level Two, Level Three, and Level Four classes. On the second page, he wrote a large scribbled message:

"Please make copy of your Application to Proceed. We will discuss this paper."

At the end of the second page letter, he wrote:

"Dear Marion Maureen, meet me in Room 212 at 2:30 pm next Saturday. We must have another conference.

Sincerely, Your teacher, the Professor."

I asked myself, "What now?"

* * *

I was early again. He was seated at the same long table. He stood when I entered and I sat across from him as before.

"Ah yes, Ma-ri-on, let us see what we have to do here. Do you think it possible, if I request from you, two more Applications to Proceed for me before classes begin again next week?"

"Professor . . . " I stammered.

I could feel the heat on my face and my hands begin to sweat. I knew I had to think and talk fast. Maybe I needed to take one huge big breath, like a singer building to a crescendo. I wished I could be a quick thinker.

I began my fast talk.

"Professor, I thought my paper might seem a bit elementary and since you have so many students, much more advanced than I, I confess I thought about trying to write something more intellectual. I know my writing is simpler than the others. But, I lied to you when I said I had a learning problem. I did have a problem with the computer but I'm learning quickly. I have another computer class scheduled and have a young student to help me with the formats and the other things I need to know for your class. Please forgive me for misleading you. It's that I am not as formally educated as others in your class. While I might have felt dumb, I am not. What would you like me to do to improve? I would be happy to rewrite the Application you have. Is it necessary to write two more before classes begin next week? But, if it's what I must do to progress to Level Two, I'm willing to do whatever it takes."

I was talking as fast as the Professor had talked the first day I saw him. The faster I spoke, the slower his movements became. He leaned back in his chair and peered at me again. There was a slight smile on his face. I had begun to like this young man. I wanted desperately to stay in his class.

He was very serious and spoke slowly.

"Ma-ri-on, I sense urgency in your writing. I know you are not lacking in intellect. We are here to learn to be writers. You have shown me you wish to write. You have worked hard. Are you interested in university credit hours and a degree or are are you in my classroom to learn to write and take the Novel Writing courses with the intensions of progression to the Advanced Seminars?"

Why is he asking these questions? No more lying, Marion. Tell the truth.

"It's my sincere desire to advance as far as I can. I must write my novel. I need your help. If you think

I need to write two more Applications to Proceed in order to move on to the next level, then I'll begin when I leave here today."

"Ma-ri-on, this is what I have to offer. Each semester, if I see a student who may advance faster than others, I allow the student to advance on an escalated scale. The student must do all the work in all levels of the Novel Writing course. If you wish to write for all three levels and attend more classes, you may do so. You must write all the assignments in each level. First write your Applications to Proceed to Levels Three and Four. It is very hard work. You have shown me you are not afraid of hard work. And I sense we have urgency between the two of us. I want you to write your book, also. It is a novel that is very believable. Let us see what we can do with it. If you wish to proceed."

"Oh, yes, I can do it. I want to do it." I spoke to him with self-assurance but in reality, I was wondering how this surprise might fit into my family life.

"Well then, Ma-ri-on Mau-reign, let us see how we can manage this opportunity."

My heart was beating so fast, it frightened me. I couldn't have a heart attack now. *I need to get in better*

*shape. This man is going to put me through life-shaping
events. In every way.*

I said a silent prayer,

*Thank you God, for the opportunity. Neil, you picked
the right path. I can write your book. We have work to do.*

Soon, there began an almost unbelievable
adventure. I had a promise to keep. I hadn't overcome
all my fears of the Professor or my sense of inadequacy
but I studied very hard and felt better about my
progress. My worries of the time-consuming classes
and hours of preparation were unfounded. Dan was
working hard, expanding his veterinary clinic and
handling grief in his own manner. I'd thought we'd
never been closer. We were strong for each other and,
together, we became stronger individuals. At least, so
it seemed.

Austin had married a lovely young woman and they
were expecting their first child. Heather accepted her
dream job as a teacher in the school system where
Patrick and Kellie attended. She was strong and an
excellent single parent. Travis and his family were
doing well in Iowa. Life was not easy but we were
moving on. I kept searching for strength from Neil.

ఴ

As I wrote the novel, wonders happened. Neïl's dreams and plans became my dreams and plans. I wrote, taking notes while listening to the radio. I wrote while attending the symphony. I wrote as words and music seemed to come from within a huge circle of life surrounding me. I found synchronicity in unexpected places. Music, writing, and nature, just as Neil had hoped.

I watched the sky for Jonathan and saw him many times, circling the university campus. I wondered if some student was feeding him or if, like the real Jonathan Livingston Seagull, he was the fastest flying gull in the sky.

In my writing class, once I progressed through Level One and when the Professor made it possible for me to join Levels Two, Three and Four, at the same time, I entered a world I'd read many writers enter. I was some-where between no where and now here. I was living the parts in the novel because I was a part of the novel.

There were no more hall meetings with the Professor. He did ask me to stay and have lunch with him one day.

New Beginning

Every beginning is a consequence.
Every beginning ends something.

– Paul Valery, French Poet

W<small>E MET AT A BUSY</small> Mediterranean café near the university. He was there, talking to the manager. The Professor was a regular, the staff knew him well. He sat with stacks of papers sitting on top of his tote bags. I'd recently heard the combined number of students in his various levels were more than two hundred. It wasn't difficult to imagine why he hadn't a clue I was Neil's mother. Since I'd been attending three of his writing levels, students seemed to come and go. Different faces and names read on different days.

"Ah yes, Ma-ri-on, thank you for coming." He began to collect the papers and separate them into each tote bag. After our pleasantries, I said, "Professor, I've wondered about the tote bags. Do you use them as a file system or some way you separate our assignments?" He had at least four each time I saw him. Today there were only three.

Early on, I'd followed his lead. Tote bags seemed to me to be a good way to keep my books and assignments. I'd stuffed file folders filled with my writings and a pencil box filled with pens, a small stapler, and paper clips. Not many in the upper levels carried brief cases or even backpacks. Colorful bags had become a distinguishing factor of students in his writing courses.

"Yes, they are my filing cab-in-ets. My friend in New Delhi made them for me. My wife and I think they are lovely. I have one for each class. I look at many assignments each day. I know the class by my bags. These bags belong to your classes, Ma-ri-on. This is why I requested our meeting today."

He pushed three full bags aside and opened the menu; he didn't look at me and made no attempt to say more about our meeting. He perused the laminated pages. Even though I could tell he had been there many times and knew exactly what he wanted, he began to tell me what he liked.

"The tabouli and baba ghanoush are delicious. For meat, I recommend the gyro sandwich on pita bread. Greek salad is good but the fattoush is better."

The pungent aromas of spices, vinegars, and Turkish coffee suddenly made me extremely hungry. I wanted to pinch myself. I was there with the young university teacher. Had he been Neil's friend? He was barely older than Neil, maybe they had met at this very spot. I wondered.

I listened to every word he said. I was learning to understand his accent and I hung on to his every word. I wanted to believe he had become my friend and mentor. Could that be possible?

"I'll take your suggestions and have the tabouli and fattoush salads."

He motioned to the waiter and gave him our orders. We were served iced tea. The waiter called him Professor too. Since that first day in class when he wrote his name in his unique illegible scribble writing and he'd explained we should refer to him only as Professor, I'd not heard a single person call him otherwise.

"Ah, yes, Ma-ri-on. I have an opportunity for you. I have the need to begin an Advanced Seminar next week. Earlier than usual. I wish to select a few to enter the Seminar. We must work closely to continue our works. The works this class will do has potential to reach completion. I wish to work with these few. We will forget all other assignments and classes and work diligently on our novels. What do you think?"

I leaned on the table, put my elbows on the red and white-checkered tablecloth and rested my chin on my hands. I looked at him and said, "When do we begin? Just tell me what you want me to write and where to show up."

"Good, good. Then, we will continue our important works. All your classes will be grouped into the one Advanced Seminar. We will be working only on our novels."

It sounded as if he would be writing a book too. I dared not ask. He'd been surrounded in mystery most of the times we'd talked.

"Ma-ri-on, this will be a very important class. It may well be the class that will proceed to authorship. We must take our work seriously." He repeated, "Ah yes, we must continue to create our important works."

"Does that mean no more Applications to Proceed?" I wanted to take my words back the instant I said them.

"Ma-ri-on, our lives must now be our Applications to Proceed. We will write one word, one sentence, one paragraph, and one page at a time. If the words are worthy, if they are memorable, we have passed our applications to proceed. We go to the next page. We will proceed to conclusion in the new class."

He said he was born in India and came to America after attending universities in India, England, and Scotland. I said I was born and stayed in a small Texas town until I married my childhood sweetheart. We talked about my early days in his class. He said he thought of me then as an enigma.

"Ma-ri-on," he said, "I could never understand your fear and why the unnecessary excuses. Do you want to tell me about all that?"

"No, sir, not now. Maybe some day, after I finish my novel but not now."

"No problem, Ma-ri-on, writers have secrets. I have one myself. I will tell you mine soon."

I reminded myself that I had considered him an enigma, too. We were, then, teacher and student. In the café, it seemed we were becoming friends and I had discovered my mentor. His wise interior was showing through.

I'd found a link to the bridge. Neil was right. He knew I would learn to do my part as I wrote our story.

The Professor would see me to the finish.

I was pensive and gave thanks as I left the café. I saw him to be a wonderful man; I looked forward to the years he would be teaching me to write. Seven years was beginning to sound too short a time.

Several inexplicable things happened that weekend after my lunch with the Professor. I was in a strange mood. Good news about my novel writing class usually sent me directly home to my computer. As always, when I got into the van, I turned on the radio. There was an instrumental playing from an album by the Chieftains. The title of the album was *Reel Music*. I immediately remembered Neil had liked it. It was filling my car with memories. I somehow knew the music was for me; however, I couldn't help but question if I'd ever see a bagpiper as Neil promised when he was making his plans to stay connected. I was beginning to wonder if Neil meant he'd send the music on the radio and not the real thing he talked about. Maybe sending a real person would be really difficult. Maybe I was in another non-believing mood again. It was hard to stay in the moment all the time, waiting and looking for anything that might seem to be sent by a spirit.

Neil had said, "And at very significant times when there can be no doubt of something important, I'll send you bagpipes." He promised serendipitous feelings in writing and even mystical messages heard through music. Signs in nature.

I told myself I was too caught up in my class work and not paying attention to the inner world. Maybe I was also missing things that might appear in my outer world.

That mid-day Saturday afternoon was cloudy. Heavy rain was predicted. Even so, I felt pulled to stop at a campus sidewalk flower shop. I carefully picked out fresh flowers for home and more for Neil's resting spot in the cemetery. I thought I'd get the same kinds of fresh cut flowers for each place and Neil and I could enjoy a celebration, of sorts, for my advancement to the top writing seminar. I thought Neil would surely be pleased and yet, I reminded him, I would need his help.

I kept a little duffle bag in the back of my van for such things. It held the things I might need for arranging flowers. Scissors, floral wire, ribbons, green floral foam, and several bunches of silk flowers I'd removed from the urn attached to Neil's bronzed memorial plaque. I'd usually clean the silk flowers and use them again. Since writing classes, I'd not done much to keep up with daily or weekly tasks. My duffle bag also held seasonal decorations. Little signs, Happy Valentine's, Merry Christmas, and a Thanksgiving turkey sign along with a stuffed bunny rabbit were there as I shuffled around the interior to check what I'd need before buying the cut flowers. I didn't often get fresh cut flowers but when I did, I tried to pick out the longer lasting ones.

I left the flower shop with two groups of summer bloomers mixed with some dried flowers to make the arrangements more masculine. Neil was not wild about roses but he'd always enjoyed my arrangements of wildflowers and dried weeds.

I placed the colorful flowers in the back of the minivan and headed for Memorial Gardens Cemetery, rushing against the dark skies and possible rainstorm. The aroma of the flowers mixed with the air conditioning in the van smelled so sweet I could almost taste them.

I'd wanted to feel overjoyed because of my newfound success with the Professor, but I'd begun to feel an ominous uneasiness. The closer I got to the cemetery, the darker the skies became. The radio was playing one of Neil's favorites, Mariah Carey singing "Hero." I smiled because I felt Neil knew I was coming. I sang along with Mariah, "You don't have to be alone . . . if you look inside yourself . . . the hero is in you." Neil loved that song. His younger brother, Austin, recorded it for him so it would play over and over.

I arrived before the rain. I walked to his large bronze marker; it was one of those flat ones, against the ground, not one of the big standing headstone types. We needed to get a flat marker because there were many words I wanted to write on it. I'd spent months writing a message that would last beyond my lifetime. I'd seen something like it when we were on a vacation years before. I think it was on a monument or someplace, not in a cemetery. I'd written some of the words on that day, long before we considered losing a family member. Somehow the wording of the memorial touched a nerve in me and I'd made notes. I'd found the notes when I needed words to write on Neil's marker.

I looked at the marker and read out loud, as if to check, once more, the words were as I'd meant them to be, what we'd wanted his children to remember.

Corneilius Bailey Galloway

March 2, 1957   December 31, 1994

Future times may not know how fine a life
this simple stone commemorates.
His sense of eloquence
His wit and wisdom may fade
But he lived for reasons more durable than fame.
In love of his family, his beloved wife, Heather
With adoration for his children Patrick and Kellie
In loyalty to his friends
His was of the highest intent
Unawed by opinion
Undismayed by challenge
He confronted life and death with utmost courage.

The light of God surrounds him
The love of God enfolds him
The power of God protects him
The presence of God watches over him
Wherever he is, God is
Praise God for this young man's life.

The marker needed cleaning, and the rains were
questionable at the time, so I went back to the van,
found my small child's broom, a little stool and the
cleaning solution to make the marker shine. I scrubbed

the bronze and re-read the marker. I thought, *Professor, you would be happy to see me re-reading my work.*

I had learned the Professor's editing and rewriting rules well. There wasn't a chance to rewrite on bronze. I was happy it still read well.

As I sat there beside Neil's grave cleaning the headstone, tears began to drip onto my cheeks. I yearned to hear from Neil. I strained looking in the sky for the seagull. A mockingbird landed in a nearby tree and began to make the sounds of other birds. Was the bird talking to me? I heard the tinkling of a tiny wind chime hanging on a limb of a young oak recently planted near one of the graves.

I had much to think about as I arranged and placed the flowers in the urn at the top of the marker. I had expected more help in writing the novel. I expected Neil to show up more. Oh, I knew Neil was always there but I couldn't help wanting more. On the other hand, if I had asked for more, it might seem as if I didn't really believe our plan was possible.

I had much to do since the Professor had moved me into what I considered his favored group. I was worried I'd not keep up with the rest of the writers. I wondered who they would be. Would I know any of them?

Then as I sat there enjoying the flower arrangement, I heard something. I listened harder. Bagpipes?

Certainly, you are imagining it Marion. You need to take a deep breath and come back into the moment.
But no, I did hear something. I heard it for certain.

I left all the supplies I'd been using to clean and fix Neil's marker. I got in the van and rolled down the windows and began to slowly drive around the cemetery. I could still hear the bagpipes. I grabbed my cell phone and asked information to dial Memorial Gardens Cemetery.

When the telephone was answered, I said, "Hello, I'm Marion Galloway. I'm out here by our son's marker. I hear bagpipes. Can you tell me if you know of a service using them now?" I knew I had to somehow prove myself sane.

The man at the other end of the phone put me on hold and came back and said, "No ma'am, Mrs. Galloway, there are no services going on at this time."

"Please check again," as I continued my slow search around the cemetery.

He left the phone again, then came back and said, "I checked with the manager and he said it may be the man who comes once a year to play by his loved one's grave site."

"Where is that? Could you give me the directions? I want to find him." Just as I spoke those words, I saw a man attired in full dress kilts, slowly walking and playing the bagpipes in an area known as The Grove. He was in the most beautiful part of Memorial Gardens. I managed to get out of the van and walk to the nearest bench and sit down. Amazed, I listened to the piper play several tunes. He looked directly at me and began playing "Danny Boy," one of our favorite tunes. He bowed when he finished and immediately began "Auld Lang Syne," Robert Burns' memorable tune. Neil died on New Year's Eve.

It was early summertime in Memorial Gardens.

The piper looked very old. He was unsure of his footing as he stumbled on the rough areas between the graves. I heard sadness in the lilting sounds of his pipes. His body movements seemed to be in touch with the sounds; mourning was evident as I looked at the scene. Tall but bent, I thought he looked a proud man. I gathered my strength as he began another of our songs, "Amazing Grace." I stood up and motioned for him to come my way. He nodded but kept slowly walking the same path he'd been following. I could see he was crying. I was crying.

In my heart and mind, I heard Neil's instructions again.

"Mom, when there is something undeniably important, something you must know, I will try to send bagpipes."

I wanted to talk to the old man but he made no effort to come my way. He kept playing as he walked to another driveway across the area from where I was parked. He put his pipes in his auto and slowly drove away.

I watched him go. I thought about chasing him through the cemetery but felt he wanted no connection with another person. He obviously had made the connection he cared about. But, did he know he had made it possible for me to feel the love of my son and realize something very important was about to happen in my life?

As he rode away, the rain came in a light mist. The sky darkened again and I expected it to storm momentarily.

I went back to Neil's resting place, hurriedly checked the flower arrangement, picked up my things and rushed home in a heavy rainstorm. I wanted to write about my bagpipe encounter. I thought it was what I had to do. But I'd had no message. I didn't know what to write. I felt an unexplainable bout of sadness come upon me. I tried to shake it off but it stayed with me the entire time I prepared to go to the summer Advanced Seminar on Monday.

I purchased a new tote bag. Freshened my pencils and bought new pens and lined yellow legal pads to use for taking notes. The Professor had left no instructions as to what to expect. I gathered everything I thought I would need. Still, I was more hesitant to go to the Advanced Seminar than I had been the first day at the university. I told myself I would need to get hold of myself. The Professor would not like my apprehension. There was no need to worry, I thought. After all, there would be no more Applications to Proceed. The Professor had said we would work on our novels, we would continue until completion.

I'd seen a bagpiper, heard him play important music. There could be only good times ahead.

* * *

The Professor was late to our first class. I recognized most of the students. I counted seven of us. Three men and four women. We smiled and looked at the clock. Had he forgotten? That didn't seem to be possible. We sat in silence.

When the Professor arrived, fifteen minutes late, he looked different. He was wearing house shoes. Maybe that's why he shuffled as he slowly walked into the room. Maybe he had hurt his foot. His clothes were baggier than I'd remembered.

He slid one tote bag and a zipped plastic bag on his desk. The plastic bag was the one I had seen him dig around in for aspirin. If there were other things in the bag, I never saw them.

He knew each one of us and gave a nod to us individually. He immediately began as he often had,

"Let us see what we have to do here. Today is an important day. I am going to teach the class a four-letter word. The word is BOOK. It is the book that must take precedence in this class. You must continue to write the narrative. It is the truth and beauty we seek as artists. Don't hold back. Go for clarity without compromised emotion. Art is the great ability to create balance. Be visible. Find realistic names. Always seek balance. Always seek. Don't be afraid of not writing. Write. Out of poetry comes fiction. Do not be afraid to talk about what you are afraid of."

I was writing as fast as I could and wondering what was happening in his lecture. It was unlike any other. Most of the students were not taking notes but seemed fascinated with his new style in the Advanced Seminar. I continued to take notes, trying to catch his every word.

"I couldn't wait to come to class today. Things are evolving in a pattern. Everything is coming together. Action and interaction, working together. Reading. Coming to this class and evolving is enormous."

He pulled a bottle of water from his plastic bag and held it high and drank as if he had been in the desert. Half the bottle was gone when he put the cap on and returned it to his bag.

"A good story is all that matters, it doesn't matter what the category the story is in. Tell a good story and constantly the story breaks through. It comes as success. You have one individual, the writer, interacting with society, then you have two people, the writer and the reader, and you have interaction."

He peered at me. "Many things are in you that are interesting to the reader but the writer is unwilling to let go. I am waiting for the group to have success. Let go of your self-consciousness. Hold on to the clarity and you are there. Any actions you do and what you do in terms of action, set it down gently, and don't intimidate the reader. Desire to make an impression. Always try to create a work of art. Say, you have a certain thing to write and certain things to do here and get to it. You can engage in control and still please the audience. Attempt to make it perfect."

Whoa, Professor. What is going on? This is not a regular session. I will really need to be on my toes during this Seminar. Neil, we have a real challenge here.

"Look for the strangest things. Look for the element of surprise and take the premise and provoke the reader. Make your writing provocative and credible at the same time. Always think about bringing diverse things together. Take things that have been said before and make me see. Make me understand and see and make me want to go along with you. When you let go, the reader and I will want to go with you. We will be partners."

He stopped short, almost in the middle of a sentence, and looked at the schoolroom clock behind his chair. "This will be a break time now. When we return, I will tell you about another opportunity for each of us. An overview to see the trees through the forest."

The group looked at each other. Taking a break early was not like him. But, this was a new class and things were certainly different. He wasn't taking care with his appearance today. He looked tired but was talking fast, a mile a minute. We headed for the restrooms and the soft drink machine. I noticed he went out the side door. *He's never done that before.* The group had little to say to each other. Small talk. I, for one, was wondering what would happen next. I remembered my encounter with the bagpiper. Neil had promised to send a bagpiper when there was something important, undeniably important.

After break, our Professor began again, but in a totally different tone.

"Ah yes, write, write, write. I really want these books. Enrich your work and we will continue."

He paused for more than a minute. I thought I saw a tear in one of his dark circled eyes.

Then, it came.

Tenderly, carefully, my Professor said, "Class, friends, let us see what we must do from today forward." He hesitated. "I have completed my tests at the cancer hospital in the medical center. I was admitted yesterday. I have cancer." He adjusted his posture and sat a bit taller. "I have asked permission to move this seminar from the university to the hospital. I have been given permission for a select few to continue with me. We must meet in groups of no more than three. One person at a time may be necessary. I am told I will be living behind a glass wall. We will talk through a telephone. We will see each other but talk on the telephone."

"I will be receiving a bone marrow transplant. I am fortunate to have relatives coming from India. There will be times when I will be released from the hospital. When that happens, our group will meet here, in this room. You will be notified when to meet and where. You will receive your hospital schedules in the mail. All other levels and classes will be dismissed for the time being. They will meet with me when I return to all my classes in the fall next year. There is no need to worry. We will continue our important work in this group."

The key word was *continue*. I know I blanched in color. His voice was too familiar and too courageous. He was making plans to overcome and recover from his illness. I felt sick to my stomach. I was overwhelmed and full of memories. *Please let this be a huge mistake. He is young and has a family. He is so wise, brilliant.* This can't be happening to another young man. I thought Neil had a plan for me. The Professor was a part of the plan. *Please God, let this be a mistake.*

The Professor kept talking and I kept taking notes. I don't know how I did but I knew I must.

"Your assignments will be to write your novel. You will also write a one-page paper on your reflections of your classes and another one page paper showing your problems with your novel. I will read and correct as always. You will bring your assignments to the hospital and read no more than five pages of your novel to me. You will write as much as possible and take these assignments as seriously as you can so we can complete."

When the class was over, the small group gathered around our teacher, talking, uneasily smiling, asking questions, and telling him they would be with him wherever and whenever he wanted to meet. My classmates were the bravest group I'd seen. Withholding true emotions, they were there for him.

I stood in the back of the line and waited until the last person was gone. As he turned to go out the door, I inched nearer to him and slightly held out my arms. He was taken back but I made an instant attempt and gave him a brief tender hug. I could feel his body shake and then, relax slightly. I felt he might cry. I was trying to be brave, too. I fought my desire to break and run.

I said, "I know, Professor, I do know."

He said to me, "I know you know, Ma-ri-on Mau-reign. You have great empathy for others. You show it to me in your writing."

We were in the university hallway again when he said, "Please try to keep your time with your Professor."

"Of course, Professor. I'll call you and always be there at the best times. I love your classes and will go where you ask."

"Thank you, my friend."

I shook with fear each time I entered the same
doors at the same hospital where our son, Neil, had
once entered. The Professor met several times a week
with the seminar group and sometimes he met us one
on one. Before surgery, he had first to undergo
treatments. He lost his hair, lost weight and looked
paler than when we first met, I was shocked at his
resemblance to Mahatma Gandhi. The Professor's
appearance strangely added credibility to him, yet,
his hair loss made me think of my other teacher, Neil.

Soon, he had his bone marrow transplant and we
students found ourselves visiting the Professor, as he'd
promised, outside his glassed-walled isolation room.
I had no idea the precautions taken by the hospital
when patients were in the ward reserved for bone
marrow transplants. We had to sign in and be escorted
to the window in front of the Professor.

When he was behind the glass walls and spoke
over the telephone, still peering at me, I studied
his face and body movements for hopeful signs of
improvements. First he stood by the phone, then he
sat in a chair and later, more often, we found him in
his hospital bed, too weak to stand and face us. Sadly,
the signs of improvements didn't come. Classes in the

hospital ceased. Yet, personal visits between the Professor and me continued. He was moved into a private room to another floor and another isolation ward. There were no glass walls but each visitor had to scrub and put on yellow gowns, plastic gloves, and a mask. The visitors could stay for only a few minutes. There was no time to talk of personal things or of my reasons for taking his classes. He said over and over, "Complete your book, Ma-ri-on. Do it for yourself and me. I need the book."

A month or so later, there were days he could go home and then return to the day care section of the hospital. His family always surrounded him. I knew all about that. And I understood when there was no chance for us to talk alone. It was as it should have been.

With no classes, my daily worries focused on visits to check on my friend. Thoughts of his illness consumed me. I had stopped writing. I had closed down to almost everything. I heard the music on the radio and all around me. I heard our important songs, I knew the songs were sent to me from Neil but my mind and heart were aching. Nothing helped. I felt guilty and alone. My family was worried about me. I was in that other world again. There but not there.

Then, one day when the Professor was in the day care unit of the hospital, a member of his family keeping vigil by his side asked if I would stay with the Professor so the sitter could get something to eat. I agreed to help out. I fearfully thought it might be the only opportunity I would have to tell the Professor about Neil and why I had taken his classes. I hoped there would be enough time and that nothing I'd say would upset him. I carefully structured my words.

"Professor, do you remember a student you had about four years ago? Neil Galloway?"

"Of course, Ma-ri-on, he was a favorite. Oh, so excellent a young man and writer. A friend. I couldn't believe he died. I called his law office three times because I thought there had been a mistake. I often have looked for a replacement for him in my classrooms. He was gifted. He was fun."

The Professor stopped and looked struck by an idea. "Are you two related? Galloway?"

"Yes, sir. I am Neil's mother."

He gathered his strength and sat upright in the bed. His pajama shirt was unbuttoned and he looked even more like Gandhi. He stared at me with those dark circled eyes. "You are his mother? Why did you not tell me this before now? I would have liked to have known, Ma-ri-on." My Professor repeated, "I would have liked to have known. I should have known. It is unfair to keep a secret of such meaning." He fell back into his bed and folded his pillow so he could see me better.

I had not thought he would feel so slighted or upset. I pulled my chair closer to the bed and touched his sleeved arm. "Professor, I couldn't tell you. Neil made me promise not to tell until I finished our story."

"This novel you are writing, is it true, Ma-ri-on? It has touched me. I did not know you were his mother. Never. It is curious you did not tell me. There is no family resemblance. None. You do not look alike. He was so tall, you are so small. Nothing is the same."

"There are many things the same about us." I said, "Neil and I agreed we would write a secret book together with your help. When Neil was making plans to stay with us in his spirit, he selected you to help me become a writer. Neil is my Muse, Professor. You are my teacher. I am Neil's ghostwriter. The plan was to construct a bridge between us so that we would be forever connected through writing, music, and nature.

The book was to be for his family and others who would appreciate such a plan."

My Gandhi-look-alike didn't seem to hear a word I was saying. He looked out the door of his room. He looked perplexed and worried. I was greatly sorry I had told him. I thought I had made the biggest mistake of all the mistakes I had made with him. A long period of time passed and he still didn't speak. He shut his eyes and put his hand to the brow on his head.

"I'm sorry I didn't tell you, Professor, I can see you think it was unfair. Will you forgive me?" I was devastated. I felt he might think I was heartless. I wished he would speak. He finally said,

"Dear mother Ma-ri-on, this is not a time to worry about forgiveness. There is nothing to forgive. I felt a great loss when Neil died. I looked many times for him to surprise me and come back into class. I was looking for your son when you came into my classroom. I had no idea you were his mother. It was better. You made your way without telling me about Neil." He sighed deeply and shut his eyes; I could see dampness under and around his lids.

"I was looking for Neil and I found you, his mother. I didn't know."

"Professor, I was looking for Neil and I found you."

"Ah yes, I think these have been circumstances that may appear complex or upsetting. We will look upon this situation as a gift from God. We will look upon this as a blessing. We must continue with your works. There are times when we need helpers to guide and assist us in doing things we are not able to do on our own. This is one of those times. You must look to your Muse. Your teacher is ill. I must look for serenity. You too must do the same."

I realized I could be listening to the last lecture of a man whom I'd found to be a wise and exceptional human being. Words escaped me.

More than three years after Neil died, our beloved teacher, my mentor, our professor died at the cancer hospital. I was stunned. Stunned into deeper silence. The music disappeared. The words disappeared. I closed to all spiritual possibilities. I tried to work alone. I tried to find other classes. I tried meeting with my university classmates when they regularly gathered without our teacher. Nothing worked. I was ready to quit. I was lower than low.

I am a man of travel
Torn and battered I did trod
On the road to eternity
Around every bend, I met a new friend
But never did I find such a friend as you.

Connecting our road
There was a bridge between us
You see, God helped build it.

Alone you stood and alone I walked
And then you crossed the bridge.
I asked to stand awhile with you
And you said, sit neath a shade tree.
We talked and reminisced
We learned the secret of the bridge.

We are two traveling now
No longer torn or battered
We are bright and light
We stand at the edge of eternity
And send love across with all our might.

Found on a legal pad in a briefcase
Belonging to Neil Galloway
1994

Kicked Out of Class by Life!

In order to arrive there,
To arrive where you are, to get
from where you are not,
You must go by a way wherein
there is no ecstasy.

– T.S. Eliot.

I TOLD DAN I COULDN'T
finish the book. I cried until I could no more. I thought
Dan might want me to forget the entire thing, but he
didn't. One early evening when I was particularly sad,
Dan suggested we go to our favorite Italian restaurant
located off the Interstate. He took me in his arms and
tenderly told me he loved me and that we could find
our way through all our difficulties as long as we were
together. I felt safe and secure there with my best
friend, my husband who was trying to heal me with his
love. Later, I felt it was selfish of me to think he was
saying the words just for me. I wish I had given the
same concern for his hurt, his private and terrible,
heart shattering grief.

We went to Patellio's, ordered, and had a leisurely
early dinner.

We talked head to head and wiped our tears. When

we got to my problem with the book, I said, "You know, Dan, if this whole idea was real, why is it there are so many setbacks? And where are the signs now? When the Professor died, did Neil quit? I know I shouldn't expect more. I've had so much but where is he? Maybe it is time to let go." *I know I can't but Dan wants to hear I'm thinking about trying.* Dan patted my shoulders as we were leaving the restaurant. We walked to the van and, for some reason, Dan didn't get on the Interstate. He drove around through the parking lot and went out onto a back street behind Patellio's, past a schoolyard. I didn't care which way he went home and he didn't seem to know why he was guided to go that way either. I was looking out the side window when Dan said, "Marion, look!"

We had our windows rolled up and the air conditioning going in the van. I turned my head and looked at the fenced, deserted school parking lot. I gasped at the sight of a bagpiper walking in circles.

Dan said as he began to look for the entrance, "I guess we'd better find a way into the parking lot, don't you think?" His jaw and mouth dropped open after he spoke. Dan was ashen faced. He didn't wait for my answer and found the entrance to the fenced school lot. He was intent on his discovery. He drove to a stop near a red sports car. We rolled down our windows and listened to the piper. The man with the bagpipe was alone on the lot and was certain to know we were watching him but he continued playing and walking.

He was a young man, wearing a baseball cap, dressed in casual clothes. He played his bagpipes for a long while. He looked our way when he stopped, took off his baseball cap, swiped it across his middle as he stood at attention and then took a bow. Dan and I clapped loud and smiled.

Not complete with his routine, the bagpiper continued to play another set of music. I looked at Dan. He was still pale. I fought back my emotions although there was not a doubt that we were there at that particular time to receive something.

The piper strolled to our car as he played. When he reached Dan's window, he stopped and asked, "Do you folks like bagpipe music?"

Dan moved his head in an up and down motion. I wondered why he couldn't speak. Disbelief? The man *was* a bagpiper and it was an important time for us. No question in either of our minds that he was for real. It was too much for us to take in at that moment.

I answered him, "Yes, we do like your music but it is more than that. We have a special reason for being interested in seeing you this evening."

What a strange thing to pop out of my mouth. What was I thinking? The man had no idea who we were. He was a young man no older than our sons. He was handsome and trim. I wanted to take a chance and tell him about Neil and us.

"We're the Galloways," I began, "Our son died more than three years ago and he loved bagpipe music. We are reminded of him when we hear bagpipes and it doesn't happen often. Not too long ago I heard one in Memorial Gardens, where our son was buried."

The piper gave me a sad look. "I'm very sorry to hear about your son. I sometimes go there to play my pipes. It is peaceful and cool. How old was your son?"

"Neil was thirty-seven. He was married. There are two wonderful grandchildren, Patrick and Kellie."

"That must be very hard. I'm near his age."

The three of us had touched a chord with each other. I almost felt in a dream. We were talking to another bagpiper. The first one left me in the cemetery wondering and not feeling completely connected. I guess it was more shocking and disbelieving than the one we were seeing now. I had never come across two bagpipers before. No doubt our son was with us.

The young man offered to show us the parts of his bagpipe and wrote down the name of a man who knew bagpipe history. "You know, bagpipes have a mystical history." He was eager to tell us about his instrument and where he had played it in the city. He played with the Police Bagpipe Band and on special occasions. We could tell he was an accomplished musician.

He was also easy to understand and had a knack for conversation. He soon asked, "What did your son do?"

Dan and I replied in unison, "He was a lawyer." I added, "A fine lawyer and an honest man."

Our new friend smiled broadly. "That's interesting. I am an attorney, too. Did he practice here? Where was his office? We lawyers have a way of knowing each other or meeting at times."

Dan said, "Our son's name is Corneilius Bailey Galloway. Every one called him Neil. He was 'of counsel' to a law firm downtown. He loved real estate and banking but did a bit of everything. He knew the oil business well."

"Neil Galloway. I know the name." The bagpipe-playing lawyer was searching his memory. "Where did he go to law school?" He reminded me of Neil in some strange way.

I said, "He graduated from Baylor Law School."

"Hey, how about that. I think we could have been there at the same time. That's where I went to law school. I think he was a class in front of me. Wasn't he on *Baylor Law Review*?"

Dan and I looked at one another incredulously. "Yes. Neil was an editor on *the Review*."

"I am sorry to hear of his passing but I am happy to meet his parents. Here's my card. My office and home are near by. If you should need a bagpiper," he grinned and continued, "or a lawyer, please give me a call."

The evening was settling in and he turned to go to his small red car. I couldn't contain myself. I leaned over Dan and said, "Here is our card. Is there any way you might send us a picture of yourself in kilts with your bagpipes? I'd love to have it."

I knew he might feel it was a strange request but he took our card. He said he did have a picture recently taken at a football game. He promised to send me the photo.

* * *

Seeing the bagpiper with Dan should have been
enough to get me writing again. The man had gone
to law school at the same time as Neil. Even though
they didn't know one another, it seemed a sure sign
to both Dan and me that our Neil wanted to catch
our attention. Yet, the difficulty with having one of
those wondrous happenings was not the fact that it
happened, but that the message wasn't clear. It
frightened me because the bagpiper in the cemetery
hadn't heralded good news for me. It was devastating
news. The Professor – our mentor, Neil's and mine –
had died.

No doubts were in either of our minds. Dan and I
were together when we saw the bagpiper. Once, afraid
to mention the bagpiper in the cemetery, there was no
longer any need for me to keep the secret of Neil's
promise to send bagpipers. Neil had said if there was
something we needed to know, he'd try to cross his
bridge. Neil had failed to tell us what the sign was
about or what it would be. He only said he would try
and I should be open. Thank God, Dan was with me
and first saw the piper on the parking lot at the school.

It lent some credibility to Neil's plans. I told myself this was no imaginary happening. It seemed an unearthly signal, yet who would believe it? Dan and I had listened to the music, we saw the bagpiper, and still I wanted more. I wanted a sign for good in our lives.

I had no idea what Dan was thinking. A man of science, not one to get caught up in thinking about afterlife, Dan had been lovingly patient and supportive of my quest. I had a disquieting feeling that he wasn't as accepting of the messages that seemed to be coming to me. This time, I knew he saw and talked to the man. He had a reason to examine Neil's experiment, although I doubted if he would.

Dan was silent all the way home. I couldn't talk either. We were as distant as we'd been since Neil's death. Together but alone in our thoughts, we were trying to decipher the message of the "law school" bagpiper. I would have liked to have been lighthearted and happy. I wasn't. I was worried. After all, the first bagpiper I had seen could have been a death omen. It seemed that way. Then, I knew Neil wouldn't play tricks with me and I didn't believe in omens of any kind. Or did I? No, I didn't. I only looked for love and encouragement.

A message is a message. I'd need to discover the meanings.

Please, God, Neil, I thought, *Show me the love and encouragement that I need.*

The Crisis

A Death blow is a Life blow to Some
Who till they died, did not alive become—
Who had they lived, had died but when
They died, Vitality begun.

— Emily Dickinson

D AN AND I REMAINED quiet for the rest of the evening. I wasn't surprised when, in the morning, he left early to do his regular race walk.

* * *

Before Neil died, Dan's hobby was fishing. He had raised our three sons in the habits of fishing. Our sons and their dad loved to go together. The four guys went whenever they had free time. They went as often as they could by the lake on our farm, or any place that promised good fishing. They often found time when they could have been doing other things. They were happiest when packing the ice chests and getting their bait and rods together, readying for the adventures of another fishing excursion. No matter where, it was their favorite thing to do together. Many times, Neil was the chef. He'd cook and mix the dough bait they would use for bottom fishing. On each occasion, the bait was carefully chosen for the season or even the time of day at certain fishing spots. It wasn't unusual to see the boys scampering around a body of water, catching grasshoppers or water bugs to use for bait. They studied lake maps and the depths of the water. They'd made their hobby a study in angling.

Neil in particular was a devoted fisherman. He out-fished his dad and his brothers, leaving each in wonderment as they watched his piscatorial pursuits. All the while Neil fished he enjoyed the natural things he'd find on their outings, picking up shining pebbles from the beds of brooks and wading the cold clear rapids in the Hill Country rivers. He learned the names of the wildflowers and green ferns, and he could be found skipping flat rocks across the streams, having good times together with his brothers. His pockets were filled with special tidbits of nature when he returned home. I remembered once washing a small frog still in the front pocket of a pair of blue jeans Neil had worn as a young boy. My memories sometimes made me want to run outside and scream at the sky.

Those trips were one of many things that stopped
with Neil's illness. It was difficult for his brothers
and me to believe when Dan sold the fishing boats.
We couldn't imagine our garage without boats and
fishing gear.

After Neil died, Dan decided to give up fishing.
Austin wouldn't go fishing without Neil either. All I
thought about were the promises I'd made to Neil and
wasn't keeping. Travis was in Iowa with his family.
Heather and Neil's little children had no time for
anything other than school, scouts, band, and soccer
games. Heather knew they needed to carry on and she
was in motion at all times to do just that. The entire
family went in different directions. I didn't realize the
denial we were not showing. We didn't allow ourselves
to show our grief. Not as a unit or separately. I was so
caught up in the plan Neil had engineered for me, I
wasn't paying attention to the usual patterns of loss,
as explained in the handbooks about grief.

I should have seen trouble coming. I was blind to
all but my promises to Neil.

* * *

I thought Dan was taking his race walking to the extreme, getting up at 4:00 AM and doing a fast 5-mile walk every day. He'd even taken up bicycle riding on weekends. I wasn't worried and encouraged him to get as much special exercise as possible. He had time to spend on his exercising routines since the clinic had enlarged and continued to experience growth. Our veterinary clinic was open seven days a week. Dan had hired a number of veterinarians while Neil was ill and they kept the clinic running well under his guidance. He had stepped aside, shockingly so, from the hands-on care of the animal patients he had always loved.

In my eyes, all was going well with Dan and the rest of the family.

I was wrong. Maybe dead wrong.

The morning after we had seen the bagpiper, Dan woke me and kissed me goodbye as he left for his regular morning walk. He looked at me with his big blue eyes so like the ones our sons had inherited. I caught myself sleepily thinking how our three boys looked like Dan. Our sons had his strong, good-looking features. They were tall and athletic. They'd kept in shape long after their high school and college years.

Travis and Austin had darker hair than Neil but when they were together, there was no doubt they were their father's sons.

I expected Dan back home in time for him to go to the clinic at eight o'clock that morning. When he hadn't come home by nine o'clock, I called the clinic to see if he had planned to take the day off. It wasn't like Dan to schedule time off without telling me.

"Hi, this is Mrs. Galloway. Did the doctor stop by the clinic this morning when he was on his way home from his walk?"

His trusted receptionist replied, "No, Mrs. G. He's not here. I was just thinking of calling him to see why he's late. He's never late."

"Oh, he's out walking. I guess he decided to take a longer hike today. I'll tell him to call as soon as he comes home. Until then, please ask one of the doctors to see his patients and cover for him."

She answered, "Will do, Mrs. G. We'll handle it. He's looked tired lately."

I said, "Thanks." I hung up the telephone and sank slowly into Dan's soft lounge chair. Dan didn't carry his cell phone when he walked. He didn't like the weight of it on his waist. He said it could get wet. It was a lighthearted point of contention between the two of us. I wanted him to carry it every place he went.

I looked at the clock again. It was nine thirty. I tried to collect my thoughts and not think of bad things. I focused on whatever happenstance could have kept him from arriving home in time to go to his veterinary clinic.

At ten o'clock one of the associate veterinarians called.

I said, "He's not here right now, but could I help you? He'll call when he returns." I tried not to sound worried.

The doctor hesitated before he spoke, "Nothing we can't handle, it's not urgent, but please ask him to call when he can."

As soon as I hung up the phone, I began to shake and wonder. Dan and I had seen the bagpiper. *Please let it have been a good sign.*

I slowly walked to the front door and looked up and down the street. Where was he? I closed and locked the door, went to the table and wrote a note to Dan asking him to call the clinic and me when he returned. I picked up my purse, checked for my cell phone and went out to the garage to my minivan. As I drove to the end of our driveway, I didn't know which way to exit or where to go. I only knew I had to look for Dan. He'd never been late without calling, not in all the years we'd been married. He'd always called if there was a problem. How could I not think about our encounter with the bagpiper the night before?

First, I turned on the radio. Nothing was happening to direct me to my husband. No words from Neil. No old songs. Just a heavy rock tune. My listening station had begun playing more diverse selections recently. I couldn't have understood the words if there had been a message. There was no melody. I wondered if I should search the dial for different music but remembered Neil had selected only one station.

Next, I made the rounds of Dan's daily walk trails. He wasn't anywhere. I found myself checking the ditches and looking into the areas under construction. I drove around the neighborhood and then outside his route. I was driving in a strange pattern. All the while I was calling our home hoping Dan would pick up the phone.

Driving back and forth in circles and then expanding out again before coming back, I drove so far repeating the path, my gas tank was low. When I stopped and filled the tank, I remembered my Mama reminding me to keep my gasoline tank at least half full. Everything she did was more than full; her life was never on empty. I wished for my Mama and Daddy. They'd help me. Suddenly, the *Lion King* song, "Circle of Life" came on the radio station.

Fine, Neil. What does it mean?

If ever my car could have been on autopilot, it seemed it'd been when I found myself sitting in front of Neil's grave in Memorial Gardens. There was no memory of arriving there. I turned off the radio and sat in silence. It was time to do some self-analysis. Time to go to my Source. Never so alone, my thoughts went to God. I prayed, *please, don't take Dan from me. Help me be calm. I am afraid and I don't know if I can handle another loss. Searching for signs from lost loved ones can't be what You'd have me do with my life. Help me.*

I opened my car door and walked to Neil's grave. The tune, "Somewhere Out There," was reeling through my head. I could feel Neil. I could feel the love, just as in the song from *The Lion King*. I could feel God, our Source.

I spoke what I knew I had to say as I looked down

at the flat bronzed marker. "Neil, dear son of mine, I know we promised to write the story. And you promised to try to build the bridge. We made a good start. I joined the classes. I did my best. I've seen two bagpipers and now I'm afraid. I'm not sure what you meant in sending them when they appeared. You said important times. Last night, why was the piper there? And why is your dad not here today? I need your dad. He's missing. I'm not sure I can handle more loss. If you are out there, maybe . . . ."

My thoughts trailed off and I wouldn't let myself think what started to pass through my frightened mind.

I sat on a nearby marble bench, looked, and listened to the wind in the trees and the sounds of nature. The birds and leaves made soft noises. Little squirrels scampering around the ground and up in the tall trees were actively enjoying a peaceful day. Then, I heard nothing. I sat a long while before I looked at my watch. I was lost in the silence of the day. I had stayed longer than I expected. I called home and the clinic. It was mid-afternoon and still no word from Dan. It was time for action, but I had no idea what to do. *Pray and call our minister. Maybe call the hospitals and the police.*

I'll call our minister. He'd always been there for us. I left
Memorial Gardens a worried woman.

Darkness came and I was at home alone, waiting for
the phone to ring. I had called our minister, the police
and the hospitals. I hadn't called our two sons, Neil's
family, or our friends. Not yet. The police couldn't
declare Dan missing until he was gone for more hours
than he'd been gone. The hospitals had no record of
anyone matching Dan's description.

I'd told the veterinary clinic, earlier, that Dan
would not be in to work the next day.

Our minister, Harold, was calling every thirty
minutes or so. He'd told me he had a memorial service
to perform and was taking care of the grieving family.
I understood and waited for his frequent calls. I fought
panic with every breath.

I sat in Dan's chair in the den. The lights were on
outside and in the kitchen. The kitchen and backyard
patio lights dimly lit the den. I looked out on our
waterfall and the familiar trees and wind chimes. My
brain was frozen with fear. I had no idea what to do.

At about nine in the evening, I jumped when I saw
a figure through the glass in our back door. It didn't
look like Dan; it looked like an old man. He

frightened me. He knocked. I turned on the lights in the breakfast room and opened the door.

I was stunned as I looked at his appearance. It was my husband. Unshaven and dirty, his tennis shoes were covered with burrs and his clothes were damp. He was shaking and bent, his back was hunched and he seemed to have difficulty with his balance. I'd never seen him look so pitiful. We practically fell into each other's arms. He smelled sweaty, more than when he'd walked the marathons or returned from his many long bike rides. He looked at me through blood-shot eyes, red-rimmed and swollen. At first there were no words. We were in each other's arms and needed none. I felt he had returned from the dead.

"Marion, I couldn't take it. I – I – tried to walk myself to death. I went to the cemetery, walked round and round and then, headed down the Interstate for our country place. I thought maybe an 18-wheeler truck might hit me or I'd just drop in the weeds someplace and no one would find me until it was too late. Maybe go to the farm, drown walking into the lake or with an encounter with the alligator." Dan burst into sobs he tried to control. There was no control this time. "There's been a hole in my heart.

I thought I would die. I kept walking until I thought about you and Neil's children, and about our entire family being alone. It was even worse then, none of us should be alone again, not until we are called by God. My death wasn't the answer. I turned 'round and came back as fast as I could." Dan pulled a filthy handkerchief from his hip pocket and blew his nose, loud. "I'm sorry I worried you. I should have called. I just didn't care about anything. When I came to myself, I realized I wanted to come home so we could work through this."

He continued, "After we saw and I actually talked to Neil's classmate, the bagpiper, I was confused. It was as if everything you have been trying to do was worth your trying. I'd felt so sad for you because I'd thought you were chasing a plan that didn't exist. I didn't think it could be real. Then, last night, when we were together and saw what we saw, I began to question everything. I went out to find Neil and I found only sadness and loneliness."

Dan began to cry again. I was crying too.

"I know, I know, Dan. Me, too. What'll we do? How will we get through this? Something has to change."

The phone was ringing and I turned to answer it realizing it might be our minister.

"Yes, he's home," I whispered. "He's depressed and tried to walk himself to death. We need your help. We don't know what to do."

I knew Harold would come over.

We depended on our minister for friendship and advice. He counseled us, as a minister and even more, he was like another son. He was someone with whom Dan could talk. Dan and I had a close friendship with Harold. It was more like family than minister and church members. Maybe that's what good ministers are trained to do. Training or no training, minister or not, our experience was that he'd always been there for us and for Neil during the bad times.

More recently, we had strayed from church but never were far from Harold and his family. We needed him, although we each had reservations about showing our complete and utter distress and numbness. I didn't know if either of us could concentrate long enough to make any sense at all. I knew we needed to talk to someone, because in truth, I had thoughts my life was not worth living also. It was a serious time for Dan and me. We each knew we needed help.

"You two sit down and take a deep breath," said
Harold after he came into our house and hugged us.
He was dressed in his suit, having come from planning
another memorial service for one of his church
members. Dan and I often talked about how difficult
it must be to be a minister. Harold, his wife and three
children were on display every time they left their
home. They were an extremely good-looking bunch.
Hollywood beautiful and handsome, they could pass
for movie stars. Two blonde daughters and a dark-
haired son, the girls like their mother and the son like
the father. But none of them focused on appearances.
They never showed it to the congregation. They took
their good looks and good works as gifts, I'd supposed.
In our case, we knew and loved each family member.
Harold and his wife were a source of solace and loving
care for us.

It was late, we all needed rest, but his message
needed to get through to us.

"First let's pray a prayer of thanks for your safety
and well being. Let's ask God to be with us tonight
as never before. It's not a bad thing. It's good you've
finally faced grief together. God knows and I know
how hard you've tried to protect each other and hide

your feelings. Let's try to look at this day as a breakthrough in your journey through the crisis of Neil's new path. We'll know Neil is still with us in spirit, he'll always be in our hearts and in all the ways he said he'd try to stay with the family. No doubt in my sometimes skeptical mind, Neil's love for his family has broken barriers. Your love for him has directed your lives so that, together, you have experienced wonderful happenings."

"When you wake up in the morning, accept the bridge Neil is building. May there be room for rejoicing for each memory and each time we are reminded of him. Let's know that, at times, you can walk with him on the bridge between life and death. You can live full lives yet look at the difference that has happened to you because of your loss. Think what Neil would want you to do. What would your God have you do? Listen and look to nature, to music and write your book, Marion. Dan, accept the wonders that are out there for you. I love you two. We're blessed for knowing about Neil's unusual plans. Now it's time to live your lives and do as he would want you to do."

Dan and I were glad our minister had come. I wasn't sure we wanted to hear the sermon we received.

We did, however, listen.

Before Harold left, he suggested we take off for a while, go some place different, some place we'd never been but had a desire to go. He said, in his typical leanings towards athletic talk, "You two need to take time out. The clock's been ticking too long. It's time for a break."

We thanked and hugged him. He kissed my cheek and shook Dan's hand and put his arm around Dan's shoulders and tightly gave Dan half a bear hug before he left. We'd had a very long day. We were drained of emotions.

Sleep was our friend. Dan and I climbed into bed and cuddled under the covers. We clung to each other in our safety net of love. Later, we woke and there, thinking but not talking, I found the courage to whisper in Dan's ear, "Let's go to the bookstore in the morning and look for a place to get away."

Dan answered in his typical money-conscious way, "We could use some time together but we need to remember the school fund for Neil's kids."

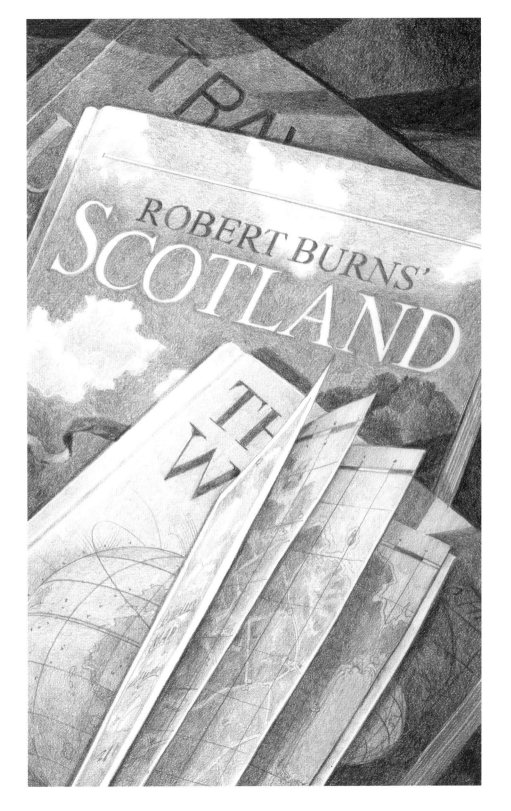

* * *

Dan and I went straight to the travel section in our favorite bookstore close to our home. We each removed numerous travel books and took them to a nearby table. I went back for more European travel books. Dan was in the United States section. We'd traveled some with our church group but never a trip abroad alone. In groups we didn't worry about language differences or places to stay. This time, with just the two of us, Dan felt we needed to be more selective.

"Marion, I don't want to go any place if we can't communicate. Let's look at the USA or at the most, English-speaking foreign countries."

He'd just ruled out my hopes for romantic Venice.

"I think you're right Dan, let's look at England and the British Isles."

Dan countered, "How about New England, we could see the colors of fall. Nice little bed and breakfast places?"

"Maybe so, I've heard it's beautiful. Do we want to plan that far ahead? Let's think about going now. As soon as possible. We need it."

I sat reflecting, maybe looking for guidance again.

Suddenly I had another one of my strange bookstore feelings; I got up and ambled over to the travel books. There, facing out on the bottom shelf, was a small, very thin, picture book. A painting of a handsome young man was on the cover. The only words written on the cover both back and front were the words, "Robert Burns' Scotland."

"Ah, Dan," I said as I took the book back to the table, "Please? This is where we need to go."

Dan looked at me and gave me a hopeless sort of sigh, "Let's think about it Marion."

We purchased the little picture book and a travel guide to Scotland. I piled guilt upon myself because I hadn't looked for a picture book of Burns' Country to show Neil while he could read and enjoy it. It crossed my mind that I was pushing Dan to do something he'd rather not do and maybe the plan was one I should mention to our minister.

The Getaway to Alloway

For you shall go out in joy,
and be led back in peace;
the mountains and the hills before
you shall burst into song.

– Isaiah 55:12

A Man's A Man for A' That – Robert Burns

NEIL HAD LAUGHED AND enjoyed imagining that Dan and I would one day take a trip around the world on the frequent flyer points our credit cards had earned while he was ill. When we would drive Neil to the many different medical specialists, he'd often remark to the doctor's personnel, "These are my parents. Please tell the doctor he is helping to send them around the world on frequent flyer points."

He loved the shocked reaction. It was true, the medical bills were horrendous. Neil had good insurance but there was twenty percent left to be paid during most of his visits to the doctors. We knew it wasn't easy for him to depend on us so much but his practice had fallen off and so had his income. He knew we were all thinking about his wife and children and were trying to make sure they would be cared for if the worst happened.

During the last few months of his life, he thought and worried more and more about Heather, Patrick, and Kellie. He knew the children were too small to understand what was happening. Neil was deeply in love with Heather. He knew she had to spend most of her time with the children and at her teaching job. She and the children were with Neil as much as they could be, but it seemed never enough. Each time they came and left, Neil was very sad.

We'd raised a strong son. He was a very devoted husband and father.

Dan and I'd cut back on our lifestyle to cover the costs not provided by insurance, and we did, when possible, try to add to our frequent flyer miles when paying Neil's remaining medical expenses. I'd hoped Neil and his family could use the frequent flyer points when he was better.

We faced some miserable times and tried to make the best of fate's stinging arrows.

* * *

Neil enjoyed reading and thinking about mythical
Scotland. It was compounded when he had a bit part
in the Lerner and Loewe musical production *Brigadoon*
when he was in high school. The songs and music
remained favorites of Neil's. *Brigadoon* tells the story
of a place that comes to life once every one hundred
years, for one day only. A place not on the map of
Scotland, an enchanted place, filled with magical
legends and beautiful music. Neil was intrigued by
magical, mystical stories.

From time to time Neil would sing, *"What a day this
has been, what a rare mood I'm in . . . there's a smile on
my face for the whole human race . . . well, it's almost like
being in love."*

His interest in Scotland and the poetry of Burns
remained with him for the rest of his life. I now think
of those years as Neil's "mid-life" years. No wonder he
savored his days as a young man. Did he have an inner
knowing? Certainly Rabbie Burns lived his life rushing
through. If I checked with Nettie, our country
neighbor, I'd bet she'd tell me Vic, Jr. lived his young
life to the fullest. I remembered Neil and Vic loved to

garden, and Rabbie Burns was a farmer. Time and again Burns returned to his farms as Neil did to his gardens.

And the Professor? Different yes, yet whirling through his young days with the same passion, reading, teaching, and writing. All family men, caring for their wives and children. I wondered if they knew their lives were directed by a short destiny. Then, gone they were. Each missing but still found and remembered in their ways.

And of Neil's dreams of one day visiting Alloway, Scotland, we'd do it for him and with his spirit. He'd wanted to visit the "auld" Brig o'Doon on the "braes" of the Doon River. We were on our way, perhaps to our destiny.

Alloway is located in the heart of Robert Burns country. As we traveled there, I thought about dreams that often leave with the winds. They come into our thoughts and vanish into stillness. I guessed they did for Neil.

We had some melancholy times thinking about his unresolved desires to travel. And there were some good times too. When Neil spoke of visiting the Robert Burns Monument, he smiled as he teased his brothers. His younger brother, Austin, had graduated with a degree in Environmental Design where he'd learned to abhor the huge sums of money spent on monolithic structures.

Neil once gave each of his brothers an inscribed university coffee mug. Austin was given a mug with an inscription: *To my brother, "No Monuments." Austin.* On the other hand, Neil's older brother, Travis, graduated with degrees in Building Construction and Land Development, and was given a mug inscribed: *To my brother, "Lover of Land," Travis.*

When I looked through Neil's legal pads, I found, among many, the following poem, written for Travis and Austin.

To my brothers:

Creation
by your brother, Corneilius Bailey Galloway

Look around what do you see?
A desert of steel and stone.
Matter it not what man thinks
For to the most splendid of man's creations,
The smallest of God's surpasses.
If you look closely you will see
The splendor of all life itself
More beautiful than the most beautiful of man's creations –
And what God has created, man has been destroying

181

And in its place, Man puts his.

He wrote a postscript, "You guys save the land and I will cover the legal battles for you. We are the Galloway brothers, the fearsome threesome."

* * *

While Dan and I talked about plans to spend a week in Scotland, I busied myself preparing for the possibility of another big event in our search for wholeness. Rather than thinking about packing clothing, I thought about Neil's writings and spent time reading and compiling my treasures before we left. I read and organized his legal pads. I wanted to get his writings in order, just in case our plane went down or we had an accident driving on the wrong side of the roads in Scotland. I wanted to be certain everything would be in place for Heather and their children if we didn't return and did so by carefully removing the pages from his legal pads and placing them in three ring acid-free plastic sleeves. I made a thick notebook of his writings and poetry. Neil was a doodler too. He'd left behind pages of little drawings and unfinished sentences. Once I had begun work on the notebooks,

I almost lost my enthusiasm for the trip to Scotland. Why go to Burns Country when I was reading Neil's poetry and notes? Instead of taking the long trip to Scotland, maybe Dan and I should drive 200 miles to the Texas Hill Country and enjoy ourselves there.

Then very late one night, when I was finishing my work organizing his legal pads and notebooks, I felt a strong desire to stop and watch TV. We'd not watched our TV much in a number of years. We did watch the weather channel. I went into the breakfast area of our home where Neil had spent his last days and turned on the old movies station. The advertisement for the next movie made me shiver. The late night movie was *Brigadoon*. I guess I'd forgotten about the movie. It was filmed in 1954, three years before Neil was born. I watched in delight. I knew the musical but had not seen the movie. The songs were as timeless as our son would always remain to us. And, I'd not remembered the one song called "Heather on the Hill." It brought back memories of Neil's love for Heather, of his high school days and more. All the reasons Dan and I should go to Scotland. I was certain we should go. I had definitely had a musical message. I wanted to wake Dan but decided to let him sleep. He'd find out when we got to Scotland. I had an inner knowing that Neil would be with us and set us on our new life path. The movie could not have been coincidental. I was meant to see it and it made me excited once again. Another Neil-inspired journey. This time Dan and I would go together and experience whatever it would be. Together.

The next morning, I began packing and reserved frequent flyer, first class airline tickets for Dan and me to make our flight to Scotland.

On the flight over, I realized Dan and I were going to Scotland for more than one reason. Perhaps we would find our lost selves there, along with a newly found way to come to grips with the loss of our son. We were flying straight into the land of musical bagpipes and mystical clans.

We landed at Abbotich Airport outside Glasgow. The flight took eleven hours including a short layover at London's Gatwick Airport. We'd arranged for an auto and were shuttled to the auto rental location near the airport. Dan had never driven on the left side of the road. He took instructions from a friendly Scot behind the rental counter.

"No problem," Dan said. He went on to say it would take him only a short while to learn to pass on the right. I hoped so. Before we left we asked about lodging near Alloway. In one of the coincidental moments we'd often had, the man handling our auto rental told us his mother had a cottage very near the Burns Monument. He called his mom and found the cottage was available. Dan and I smiled. We had our first worry resolved before we left Glasgow.

As always I was Dan's co-pilot. We felt we could make the thirty-five miles to Ayr and find the road to Alloway in plenty of time before dinner. He was doing very well driving on the wrong side of the road.

The instructions we received at the rental counter were to pick up the keys to the cottage in Ayr and ask for directions. It was easy to find the owner. A rotund friendly red head dressed in a full skirt and loose fitting blouse, she seemed thrilled to meet Americans. She'd fixed a box full of food carefully packed in individual baskets inside sections of the box. She'd covered it with a green plaid tablecloth. She explained her cottage supplied breakfast and lunch and she would bring both daily. Knowing we were tired and in a hurry, she gave us the keys, a map and sent us on

our way.

We'd hoped to spend the remaining part of the day resting in the cottage before we began to explore Burns Country. We'd left on A77 southwest of Glasgow and headed through the countryside for the coastal city of Ayr. The little city was in Burns Country and on the outskirts of the Southern Uplands. As we followed our map to the cottage owner's home, we found ourselves near the Auld Brig o'Ayr of which Rabbie Burns wrote, "Poor narrow footpath of a street where two wheel barrows tremble when they meet."

Dan pulled over by the bridge and said, "Marion, this trip may turn out okay. The place abounds with my family history. It would be nice to visit the home of our ancestors." We looked at the map and saw a nearby town called Galloway. It wasn't far from Alloway.

"Good idea, Dan. Let's try to drive around that area too, see what we can find out about the family."

Dan held my hand as we walked to the bridge, stopped and took a photograph of our first "Auld Brig." We were already learning the language for "old" and "bridge."

"I think this land is magic, Dan. No wonder musicians and poets love this place. I once read an article that said Beethoven was inspired by some of

Burns poetry. Do you think that's so?"

"Let's check it with someone while we're here," Dan said in his typical scientific "let's research" attitude.

We returned to the car and began looking for the cottage at the end of Under Mountain Road. We were told it was just a mile or so from the Burns Park and the Doon River in a little woodland at the base of a small mountain.

When we turned off the main road and onto the path that lead to our cottage, a haze was gathering at the top of the mountain. There was a waterfall tumbling down the slope near the cottage. "Goodness, Dan, look at the waterfall and the lovely garden. What a beautiful little stone cottage. It must be centuries old. It's perfect. How could we be so lucky?"

Dan was tired, "Yes it is. It's all as you say, but let's unload, get some sleep and rest up for tomorrow."

Our hostess had packed the picnic baskets full of sandwiches called *toasties*, some homemade cookies, and a tin of oatcakes. There were a couple of bottles of water, local orange soft drinks, and Scottish beer.

We had plenty to eat and noticed that the hostess had tended to breakfast by leaving fried bread and potato scones for the morning. We were set and ready to enjoy Robert Burns' Alloway.

Sunrise was trying to peek through the early morning dewy mist. Dan was eager to get out and exercise. We'd been cooped up long enough on the trip from Texas and our drive to the cottage from Glasgow to Alloway. No longer worried about Dan walking to escape from his memories, I knew he would want to explore the hilly countryside around the cottage. I also knew he'd want to spend much of our time together walking around Alloway when he returned. He was in great shape for his seventy-two years. On the other hand, since hard times befell me, I'd spent no time at all exercising. I'd sat in front of my computer or in classrooms while trying to learn to write a novel. I was happy I brought my red collapsible walking cane. Dan had packed his favorite walking stick and put on his glow-in-the-dark walking vest and athletic shoes before his early morning walk.

"Don't forget your water bottle, Dan. Do you think our cell phones will work in this little hidden meadow?"

He smiled and said, "I'll take my cell, but I doubt it

will work." He pointed toward the direction he planned to take. "I'll stay to the highland trail." We each laughed; we were sounding like Scots already.

"Dan, you need to promise me you'll not get lost and stumble on the mystical town of 'Brigadoon.' I want you back. Remember the town comes to life every 100 years. If you come upon it, don't go into town, that's too long for me to wait for you. Be careful and give me a time when you expect to return."

Dan turned around and raised his voice so I could hear him, "Who says we aren't in Brigadoon already!"

Our faces were worry free. We were readying for our Scottish adventure. It was our getaway. I loved those words, "getaway to Alloway."

It was the first time in years we'd been so jovial and unencumbered. There was something about visiting the place, finding the cottage, and settling in for three days of unplanned exploration. We didn't mention Neil although I knew we would find it difficult not to talk about him once we got to the Burns Memorial. And, strange as it was, we had not seen one bagpiper or heard traditional Scottish music since we'd arrived. Given the fact that bagpipes are known in Scotland to be exclusively Scottish, I thought we should have seen them immediately upon arrival. Maybe it was too early when we arrived at the airport.

Dan made his way in the morning mist towards the trickling waterfall and began to walk the slight slope up towards the top of the hill. He looked back at me and waved, grinning from ear to ear.

I walked back into the cottage, slipped into my favorite loose fitting sea foam blue dress and walking shoes, ran my fingers through my hair and pulled it back away from my face. The mirror showed streaks of gray mixed in with the light brown. My multicolored hair was most noticeable when I'd grab the fine strands, smoothed them without a comb, pulled tight and twisted it into a looped ponytail.

Maybe you need to get a hair cut. You should take better care of yourself Marion. You have let yourself go.

In the daylight, I took a better look at the cottage. It was charming. Made of old stones turned a grayish color during the many years it had been there, it looked like a painting, maybe an antique painting. A low rock wall surrounded the garden. The waterfall had cascading waters that pooled into a shallow pond before bubbling down into a little stream that led away from the cottage. Maybe it flooded a bit during rains;

however, it was obvious someone had planned the
setting with great care.

Alone, I wandered through the hedges, flowers
and around the back of the cottage that led to a thick
cover of bushes and trees. I stopped suddenly when
I saw a deer standing between the cottage and the
woods. A buck, he looked at me and slowly moved his
head as if to show me his tiny antlers. He was a proud
fellow. I stood without moving until he turned and
made his way to the woods. My heart was pounding
hard. I immediately remembered the deer I'd seen in
Texas on the way to our country place and as I stood
there I'd used my imagination to compare Texas with
the Borders of Scotland. It was then, and only then,
I allowed another thought of Neil.

I walked and breathed in the picture perfect
landscape. I felt so close to God and Neil, I began
to pray.

"Thank you, God, for giving Dan and me this
opportunity to understand ourselves again. Thank
you, God; he is a wonderful husband, father and
grandfather to our clan. Thank you, Neil, for being
with us all along the way. Thank you for my time with
the Professor. Thank you, God, for Neil, his wife and

children; for Travis, his wife and adult daughters; and for Austin, his wife and precious young family. I'd assumed my duty was to write the book. If it doesn't happen now, I know you'll lead me to the next step in our lives. I need to ask. Have I failed and misunderstood my mission? Is it right to continue this impossible dream, maybe a fictitious task? Am I forgetting the reasons Neil wanted to build his bridge? Did I ever know the reasons? God, help me find the message if I am to complete the book and be receptive to the bridge." I pleaded, "Please help me."

I stood with my face slightly lifted and saw an amazing sight. I was not alone. The three rays of light were back, the ones Nettie and I saw in Texas. The light rays were clearly breaking through the trees and shining on me. I never felt the presence of our son more closely than at that moment, in the garden by the cottage. I sank into the carpet of soft green grass and waited. I felt a strange warmness in the cool misty grass. The sounds of the water, the wind in the trees, the sweet smell of flowers and songs of little birds filled the air. I wished for my computer or a pad on which to write. Words were flowing throughout my being and in my mind. There was music in my heart. There was a deep knowing trying to come forth. I hoped it would stay with me and bloom and burst through in my writing.

I heard the rocks moving under Dan's feet as he came down the mountainside. He was breathless. "Marion, did you hear the bagpiper on the Auld Brig o' Doon? He was playing as he crossed the old bridge. If you didn't hear him, maybe he will be there early tomorrow and we can go see him. I got a good look at the Doon River and the bridge. It's about as big as the Blanco River in Texas. Not big at all. You've got to see it, Marion."

I said, "Let's get over to the Burns' Monument and look around."

"Done. I'll bathe and dress and we'll spend the day exploring Alloway." Dan walked past me and headed for the cottage door. "Did you have a good morning too?"

"I did, Dan. It was peaceful and quiet. Did you see the light rays when you were on the hill?"

"No, I didn't see the rays, I heard the bagpiper though."

"Yes, there was enough for me too. Let's see what

the rest of the day will hold for us."

"Let's get on with it, Marion." Dan was ever in a hurry and never one to mince words.

Dan went inside to get ready and I stayed in the garden for a while longer, savoring the feeling of being in another land. I lingered there, filled with tales of a different time. I wanted to read and write about it. I was trying to memorize my thoughts and visuals as I meditated on the beauty of the waterfall, the garden and the little hidden cottage.

Soon I heard, "Marion, can you come inside? I want to show you something." I pulled myself up with difficultly. I hadn't lowered myself onto the ground in years. My bones ached. I supposed I hadn't recovered from the trip, but in truth, I ached all the time in recent months. I wanted to feel young again but found it difficult when I couldn't move easily.

Dan was standing by a bookshelf. It was full of books about Robert Burns, Sir Walter Scott, Robert Louis Stevenson and deer stalking in Scotland. No surprise there. If we were in Texas, staying at a bed and breakfast, we'd likely find books by revered Texas authors J. Frank Dobie, Roy Bedichek, Walter P. Webb, and more recent writers, John Graves and my favorite, Leon Hale. There would be the ever-present Sportsmen's Almanac's detailing hunting and wildlife management. The bed and breakfast in Texas, as in Scotland, would likely be made of stone. I felt, in newly found Scotland, that the countries that molded generations of our families were constantly vying for my attention as I sought balance.

The little TV and video combination sitting on top of the bookshelf did surprise us. There were just a few videos. The one that caught Dan's eye was Disney's *The Lion King*. I looked at him and said, "You know, Dan, I expected more than our fill of bagpipers here in Scotland. I expected to be spellbound a time or two what with Rabbie Burns and Neil's love for the place and our new found fascination with the poet and his country. I didn't expect *The Lion King* to show up."

"Interesting," said Dan. "Maybe we'll play it tonight when we come back to the cottage."

We did not.

Our first day started with the rays of light and the bagpiper and continued to be filled with wonder. We went directly to the Robert Burns National Heritage Park, a few miles down the road off A77. Dan felt we could have walked it. I assured him I couldn't make it and still tour other sites. Our maps showed Burns' place of birth to be a tiny spot of a town. I wasn't ready for the Burns Monument. Even Austin in his critical analysis of monuments might have liked it. Spectacular views of Alloway and the Auld Brig O' Doon, bank-to-bank crossing the narrow Doon River, could be seen from the top of the monument. Inside, we found Burns' white marble bust and I did a double take. Rabbie was known to have dark hair and dark moody eyes; our Neil had light hair and clear blue eyes that held us transfixed at times. Looking at the white marble, with no care given to color, there was an undeniable resemblance to Neil. I stood there and tried to make sense out of the entire experience. I read the words of Burns' song on a brochure we picked up.

Ye banks and braes of bonie Doon,
How can ye bloom sae fresh and fair?
How can ye chant, ye little birds,
While I am weary and full o' care?

Rabbie's words reminded me of Neil's words about the beautiful Blanco River or should it be the other way

197

around? Maybe Neil's words reminded me of Burns'? Young men, they'd left their marks. Do we all search to leave our marks? Will I ever finish the book? If I do, will I then die too? It was a frightening thing to think about following in their footsteps.

Our first day of adventure in Scotland was getting to be too much. I needed to center myself and search for the reasons we were there.

* * *

The next few days, Dan and I walked and drove around the southern parts of Scotland. We didn't talk about Neil when we heard bagpipers and we heard many. They were there, we were there and Neil was there. So was his friend Rabbie, and even the Professor and Victor, Jr. We were traveling with heady company. But we didn't mention them. We knew they were with us.

Dan and I discussed our heritage and searched out information on the Galloways and the Dunlops. We found our clan tartans. I bought a beautiful shawl that was folded in a bag I could add to my tote bag collection. The Galloway tartan plaids were beautiful greens, with strands of gold and red. My clan, the Dunlop's, had colorful plaids too. Many shades of blues with darker almost black squares now and then. I purchased a Dunlop shawl in memory of my Mama, Daddy and Grandma Dunlop. I thought the tartans for each of our families were the prettiest in all of Scotland.

Each night we would go back to the tiny hidden stone cottage. It was almost as if we were in Brigadoon, and if we'd stayed, it would be 100 years before we could come back to Scotland and the real world. Worth consideration, maybe.

The three days we'd booked in Scotland flew by. The moments in the garden and at the memorial monument were soon to be precious memories. I wondered if I would write about them. Dan loved the weather and his early morning walks. I felt he had made his own special memories with Neil there in the woods and on the mountain by the streams.

On the way back to the Glasgow Airport, we wanted to make a final stop at the Irvine Burns Club in Ayrshire. We'd heard the collections there displayed stories about the poet and that we could expect to see stunning murals that told the story of Burns, the farmer, and his desires to become a businessman in retailing and manufacturing flax. Burns found himself in Irvine and when he left he hoped to become the poet, no longer in the flax business or needed at the farm. He'd found the poet in himself.

We also wanted to see a medical doctor's daybook recounting Burns' illness and of his visit with young Rabbie just before he died. It brought to mind my daddy who was a medical doctor, not long gone. I knew Daddy would be curious about Burns' doctor's notes. I was sad I couldn't tell him about it.

We were wandering around the Irvine Burns Club when I heard Dan,

"Marion, come look at this." It was the same incredulous voice I'd heard Dan use when he saw the bagpiper on the school ground in Texas, although I knew Dan would not be calling me to look at bagpipers in Scotland. We'd enjoyed many in our three-day visit. Dan was standing in front of a painting titled, "Burns and the Vision" by James Elder Christie. I couldn't believe my eyes. Christie had painted Burns with a muse above and behind his head.

One word came out of my mouth, as if Neil had it put there, "Awesome."

"Dan, would you believe?"

Dan replied, "Marion, there's no doubt, I believe. This muse thing has amazingly spoken again. Now it's time we go home. You need to finish *The Ghostwriter and the Muse*. You need to do it for Neil and you need to do it for us so we can get beyond this point."

Dan continued, "Marion, I've been thinking, for our next trip, let's go to the Texas Hill Country. Let's take all the family. We could begin saving and planning as soon as we get back to Texas. We could visit some dude ranches and find the one that would suit our family best. It'll be our anniversary present to each other and doing it that way, we'd keep the kids from wanting to throw a party for us. We'd have a real Texas celebration with guitars and hayrides, horseback riding, chuck wagon dinners and early morning breakfasts outside on the trails. Maybe teach everyone to square dance."

He looked happy again. He'd found his answer and he hoped I had, too. Scotland would always remain in our memories. Thoughts, poets and bagpipers surrounded us while we'd traveled the land. We'd always hear the music and find messages in music, writing and nature. The promise of Neil's bridge had been shown to us in many ways.

It was time to go home and complete the book. Questioning didn't seem so important to me anymore. I knew Neil was with us. I knew I would need to accept whatever came our way.

Still looking at the painting of Burns and his muse, wrapped in my new shawl, I said, "Good idea, Dan."

I was counting our family members. "Let's see Dan, there'll be sixteen of us, I think. You know, Neil wanted to go back to the Hill Country." I looked Dan's way. He rolled his eyes and didn't seem to appreciate my comment.

"Hey now, sweetheart, you don't seriously think we'll come across any bagpipers out there in the hills, do you? Impossible. Don't even mention it."

I held tightly to his arm and leaned to kiss his cheek. We were grinning again.

"No, it is not likely. Crooning cowboys maybe. 'Home, Home on the Range' and other cowboy songs. Gene Autry and Roy Rogers from long ago."

"Let's talk about listening to Willie Nelson, Jerry Jeff Walker and Dolly Parton. Our grandkids wouldn't know Gene or Roy," laughed Dan.

I couldn't help dreamily thinking to myself, who

knows what will happen during our family celebration? Neil did have that story about a bagpiper in the Texas Hill Country.

* * *

On the plane, I covered my shoulders with the soft woolen Galloway shawl. Dan was reading a book on the Galloway clan we'd purchased the day we visited the southern areas of Dumfries and Galloway. We'd found much Galloway and Dunlop history. The books on Scottish genealogy were an unexpected find. Dan had decided to further research our pedigrees on the Internet when we returned to Texas.

I dug around in my new tartan tote bag. I found and unfolded the small group of poems I'd brought from my file of Neil's poetry. I was looking for the one I remembered about the Hill Country and the Blanco River. I pulled myself closer to Dan and read in a whisper:

Beautiful Blanco Banks
I watch the rush of water from the
beautiful Blanco banks,

I feel the pains weighed upon the minds of men,
They bend the mighty wind.
Yet strong hearts stand firm
While asking why men die?
I know the pure soul will spirit be
And will know the answer why.

And another:

Why?

We ask the question and its reason
Ask why we live and be?
We exist only as dreams
To be only for the wonder of a dreamer
But, to seek the question, men will dream
And in the seeking of the question
We will find it was but a dream itself.

I carefully folded the poems and put them back in my tote bag. I felt as if the entire trip had been a dream. I bent my head to the left, hoping to find a resting place on Dan's shoulder. Maybe I could fall asleep and dream again. I didn't.

I began to think about our family. They were tugging on my heartstrings. Thinking about school

clothes needed for Neil's children brought back wonderful memories of getting our little boys ready for school, and then I remembered them as teenagers going to ball games and athletic functions. I wanted to see our entire family. Taking a trip to Iowa to see Travis and his family would be nice. Trips to the zoo with our younger families in Texas. Or picnics to re-introduce ourselves to the little ones. It had been a long time. Too long for a Grandma and Grandpa to be away from normal family activities. I wondered if they had felt slighted because of the time I'd spent on the project Neil and I had concocted.

I began writing the book in my head again. I couldn't give it up, although I realized I needed to give more attention to our other family members. I am doing my balancing act again. It was a game I'd played with myself since I began the journey after Neil's parting. I was in the world of here and now and wondering where I would find myself when we arrived home in Texas. How could I write without our Professor? Would I find another teacher? Was I supposed to keep looking for others? I'd tried for years and hadn't been able to complete the book. I had been guided through the years by untimely events as well as special happenings.

I was still trying to balance things when we landed in Texas. I was looking forward and searching to renew a life I'd put on hold for many years.

I prayed again. God, *help Neil and me, help all the family find our true path.*

The Bridge in the Texas Hill Country from the Edge of Eternity

---

There is a land of the living and a land of the dead
and the bridge is love, the only survival,
the only meaning.

– Thornton Wilder

THE TRIP TO ALLOWAY was short and enjoyable. It was almost like I imagined our honeymoon might have been. When we were married in Ida, we left after the reception to see the gulf waters near Corpus Christi about 200 miles away. We spent what little money we had sharing food with the seagulls while we camped out on the beach. A couple of nights and we were back on the road home to pack and move to College Station where Dan was a veterinary student.

Almost fifty years later, in Alloway, we were happy and more carefree than I'd remembered for years. I'd realized that I needed to spend more time with Dan. We needed each other now more than ever. We'd stayed close, made love and put forth efforts to catch up for the years we'd lost as a couple since Neil's illness began and after his funeral.

The Scotland trip gave Dan and me the break our
minister rightfully thought would be good for us. Plans
for the changes we needed to face in our lives began to
be discussed. We took steps towards recovering our
family and ourselves. All done in less than a week.
Dan and I knew we would, together, begin to be more
open to the wonders that kept coming our way. And,
we'd found a joint interest in some things Neil liked so
well. Looking back, his ideas weren't out of character
for the rest of us. All three of our sons had been raised
the same; they were readers, lovers of music and
nature. Things didn't seem to need to be so secretive
any more. Dan and I hoped those around us would
notice our example in openness. I was, once again,
open to writing the book Neil and I planned.

It was a shock when, a few weeks after we returned,
I heard myself say, "Dan, let's think about moving."

We'd been living in our home for thirty-five years.
It had suited the family well in our growing years.
We had moved there when our boys were little. Dan's
veterinary clinic and all the schools were within
walking distance. At the time, it was perfect for our
family. Back then, we'd carved a place for ourselves
and our sons in the community and the schools.

In the now, I continued, "Memories are wonderful but Dan, they're painful for me when I walk through the rooms. I can barely go into the breakfast room without seeing it as Neil's last hospital room. I don't like driving past the schools every day. Everything here brings up memories."

Dan replied, "Marion, let's not go off on wild tangents. There's much we could do to change the place here. Would you like to remodel again? You could design a better writing studio and redo the boys' rooms again, maybe make a TV room upstairs for our sons when they bring the grandchildren home to visit. The house is so near the clinic. Let's consider the business aspects of a move."

"I know, but maybe we could look for another spot, nearby."

"Marion, think about the logistics and the costs of a move. This place is paid for, I'd thought we had it fixed for as long as we stayed in the city and until we retired to our country place." Dan was gentle in his answer but I could tell he meant business. It was his nature to be caring towards his family, caring for his practice and the little animals. It was also his nature to worry about money and the responsibilities we might have ahead of us with our fatherless grandchildren.

I'd been thinking way ahead. We hadn't been to our country place in a long while. It'd been heart draining for me to go and it was obvious Dan felt the same. Our ranch was another one of those things we hadn't let ourselves discuss. I'd reasoned it was because Neil loved it so. Within a year after Neil's funeral, Dan had sold the cattle and leased the land to Nettie's family.

What is Dan talking about? Retiring out there? We'll need to discuss that more. I decided not to push it. My timing was off, for sure!

I'd dropped the discussion about looking for a new house and got caught up in planning our first family reunion in the Texas Hill Country. Dan joined in the excitement with me. We went to the bookstore and found several Texas travel guides to the Hill Country, each listing numerous dude ranches and fancier spa retreats. We studied the information, looked at the maps and decided to check out the places we liked on the Internet as well as the travel books.

Dan said, "Let's be certain the ranch has a cabin for each family. The older granddaughters can share a cabin with your dad's widow. They enjoy each other."

He smiled again. It was wonderful seeing Dan smiling so much.

"Dan, your idea is the best thing that's happened to our family in years. You know, we never had time for family vacations. Our daughters-in-law's families always had their family gatherings at the beach, the bay or at some spot away from home. True, our Gulf Coast ranch has been there for us but we haven't had the room to bed down everyone and spend a few days. I'm excited. I think we should try for a few days before and stay the long Labor Day weekend. What do you think? Maybe five days?"

"We'll need at least five cabins. All with kitchenettes and enough beds for each family member. The ranch needs a river or, at the least, a creek."

I wanted a place that was rustic and with lots of room for the grandchildren to roam with their cousins and parents. With Dan and me, too.

Dan found the place on the Internet. It had six hundred acres to explore, all our requirements and lots of cabins around a nice big compound. We decided to take a chance and go without an inspection. It would be a real adventure, like we'd had in Scotland. The first weekend in September was a good date for all the members of our immediate family.

We began including our sons and their wives when organizing for the large gathering of our Texas-born "clan." Everyone was thrilled about the opportunity to see one another and get to better know their nieces, nephews and cousins, and be with my daddy's recent widow. I was looking for some good old-fashioned fun for a change.

* * *

Dan and I left early on the day we planned to arrive at the dude ranch. I wanted to check the cabins and select ones that I felt would be best for each family.

Everyone was expected mid-afternoon or later in the day. Travis and his family were flying from Iowa to San Antonio, renting an auto and meeting us after they made a quick stop by the Alamo to offer a history lesson to their Texas-born adult daughters.

The Texas Hill Country has its particular unique beauty in early September. It's not green and lush like Scotland. It's dry, fed by little rivers and streams that run lower than in fall or winter and when landowners pray for rains to soak the area. Even so, in September, the low water rapids remain clear for the most part. It's possible to find riverbed limestone rocks in rapid waters that are actually ancient fossils. Some of the fossils are seashells and other rocks that have cast images of animals, even dinosaur's tracks. Since many of our early days were spent on my grandparents' ranch near Wimberley, we knew the joys of exploring the area around the Blanco River. Dan thought there'd be a chance our visiting grandchildren would find a piece of petrified wood or fossil rocks on our long weekend adventure.

American Indians were part of the history of Texas. On our trip to the dude ranch, Dan and I discussed taking the children on a search for arrowheads and other signs of Indian culture. I tried to turn my focus away from Neil and the fun he'd have with his young son and daughter. We'd all try to fill in the empty space for them, although it once again saddened me that he'd not be there for his children.

Dan and I drove through some of the most diverse lands in Texas, all in a span of four hours. I'd purposely brought along a travel case of country western music. I knew it would be a welcome change for everyone. Dan and I hummed along with Willie Nelson as he sang, "On the road again . . . ."

In secret and unbeknown to Dan, I'd slipped in Willie Nelson's new CD, *Rainbow Connection*. Hidden, I'd save it to listen to when the others were exploring. I couldn't stop thinking of Neil, and after all, it was Willie's newest. *Could Neil have planned that, too? Maybe a substitute for a bagpiper? Silly me.*

I had filled our minivan with food, drinks and enough supplies to feed an army for weeks. I knew I'd overdone in preparation. I didn't want anything to be missing.

We were a bit surprised when we saw the entry to the Triple Bar W. The sign in front indicated it was a top-rated, five-star dude ranch. We laughed in unison.

"What a hoot! How does a five-star dude ranch differ from a five-star fine resort?"

"How does a five-star dude ranch differ from a five-star grand hotel?" said Dan.

Certainly the answer couldn't be found in the appearance at the entrance. A nice little white limestone entrance and stone fencing faced the state highway. Native plant landscaping covered the sides of the road with an abundance of cactus and sage bushes.

We turned onto a tightly-packed gravel road

leading to the six-hundred acre ranch. We followed the rustic wooden signs to "Headquarters." A pretty young woman in jeans and a denim shirt met us on the front porch. She had a red bandana tied around her neck and a western hat dangling down her back. She leaned against a large stack of baled hay artistically placed near an old wagon wheel on the front porch. There were four rocking chairs on the porch and a huge wreath made of dried flowers and weeds hanging on the wall behind the rockers. Obviously a setting for city slickers, it was amusing to see the details used in making the place look like one would expect of a dude ranch.

"You folks are very early. Check in time is two o'clock this afternoon."

It was ten o'clock in the morning. As I'd been known to do on occasion, I began to irrationally reason with her. Younger and nowhere near as wise-looking as the Professor, maybe she'd find my excuses easier to comprehend.

"Yes, we are aware of check-in time, but we knew you wouldn't mind if we came early, set up a charge account for everyone in our group and walked around a bit, so we could check the locations of our cabins.

Our group plans to be here for five days, you know."

"Well, my boss won't be here until about noon. The cleaning staff is here now. I don't think all your cabins have been cleaned yet. I don't know how to set up an account. I'm just a waitress in the dining room. Sometimes I fill in at the desk. "

Still pressing forward, nonchalantly I made a bid for her friendship.

I said, "Oh, well. Could we come in and look around? Do you have a gift shop?"

Dan was fidgeting, "Marion, maybe we should go back to town and have a bite to eat and wait until two."

"Let's wait, Dan. I don't think it'll be necessary. I'm sure they have a soft drink machine and maybe one for snacks. We can have a picnic on one of those tables. We're Dr. and Mrs. Galloway. We have five cabins reserved. I'm happy to meet you . . . I'm sorry, I didn't get your name?"

"Yes, ma'am. Nice to meet you, too. My name is Sue Ellen."

It was if I had a grand mission and was at the university again. I felt driven to stay at the ranch and accomplish our early check-in. I couldn't leave. I had an inner knowing. I had to stay at the ranch.

Was it because I wanted to look at the cabin locations? No, there was more. *Marion, don't get started again. This is our first family reunion. Our anniversary celebration. What's going on with you? Get in balance and focus on your family.*

"Hello, Sue Ellen. That's a famous Texas name, isn't it? From TV fame on the series . . . *Dallas?*"

"Yes, ma'am. My daddy and mama liked the show."

"Sue Ellen, could we come in and look around, maybe get a map of the place so we can walk around before we check in at two o'clock?"

Dan seemed to be holding back his impatience as he listened to my insistence.

"Marion, are you sure you don't want to go into town and get something to eat? Maybe there's a book store there."

He's trying to entice me!

"Dan, I really want to stay here and wait."

"For what, Marion?"

"I don't know. I just want to stay here."

"Mrs. Galloway, why don't you and the doctor come in and I'll see if I can find the forms for you to fill out. Since there are five cabins, it will save time for my boss. I'm sure she won't mind."

"Great, Sue Ellen. We'd like to do that before we walk around."

Our cowgirl led us inside to the reception area. We sat on leather cowhide chairs while I filled out the forms. It was a room that introduced city dwellers to a cinematic-looking wild west. An inviting room full of Texas memorabilia and promises for a good time at the dude ranch.

Dan and I were smiling from ear to ear. We were convinced I'd made headway with Sue Ellen and there'd be no need to go back to town and wait.

We had no idea what was about to happen.

It took about thirty minutes to fill out all the forms. Dan wandered around inside the headquarters. He came back, sat down and began talking as I continued to write our information.

"They have a big dining hall, another room with pool tables and an old-fashioned saloon. A big bar and it looks as if they use it for ice cream and sodas like the one where I worked when I was a boy in Ida. A drug store bar. It's definitely a place for families with children."

As Dan was speaking, my ears perked. I stopped

writing and looked up.

"Dan, do hear that?"

"What? I don't hear anything."

"Listen Dan, Sue Ellen has bagpipes on the speakers or something."

I stood up and called in an urgent voice, "Sue Ellen, where are you?"

She was in the kitchen and came out in a rush. "Yes, ma'am, Mrs. Galloway? Can I help you?"

"You can. We were wondering why you put on the bagpipe music?"

"I didn't Mrs. Galloway. We don't have any music playing."

"Well, do you hear the bagpipes?"

"No, I don't."

"Dan. Do you hear them?" Dan stood and looked puzzled.

"Yeah, Marion. I think I hear something in the distance, though. Not on a speaker here. Maybe another guest is playing some music."

"Sue Ellen, do you have anyone who plays music out here, I mean a resident or guests . . . anyone? Anyone who would play bagpipes?"

Sue Ellen laughed, "Mrs. Galloway, we play

guitars and Western music and we do that when we are having a program in the evenings or later in the afternoon. We don't play bagpipes out here, never have. And yes, I do hear something. It sounds like it is coming from the back acreage. I don't think, well, I've never heard anything come from the mountain like that. Are you folks playing a joke or something?"

"Dan, let's go and see what it is. Sue Ellen may we have a map of the place?"

"Sure. I guess it's okay for you two to wander around. Don't go in any of the cabins though. I can't let you do that until my boss comes."

I was shaking like a leaf. Dan was as pale as he had been when we saw the lawyer bagpiper. Sue Ellen followed us outside on the porch.

"Calm down, Marion. Don't go rushing around; let's slowly try to figure what we are hearing."

Sue Ellen saw the cleaning staff across the field, near some cabins. She yelled at them, "Have you seen or heard anyone playing a radio or maybe music from a truck or car?"

They shook their heads, "no." They raised their arms in an "I don't know" fashion and walked towards us. One of the workers said, "I hear it too. Where is it?"

Dan slid to a seat on the steps and put his elbows on his knees. His shaking hands held up his head and he looked at me with questioning eyes.

"Sit down Marion; let's try to figure out where the sound is coming from. There are six hundred acres out here; we can't go hiking all over the place. Let's get our bearings. It seems to be coming from far and wide. How can that be?"

"Oh goodness, Dan. Neil is here. He wants to join the family. What else can it be? It can't be bad. This is a good thing."

Sue Ellen said, "Neil? Who's that? Did he arrive early, too?"

It was hot at midday in the country, but there was a nice breeze. I thought I heard a wind chime, too. I went to the minivan to find my hat and cane. Dan followed. He reached for his baseball cap and walking stick. He took the map from my hands and said, "Okay, Marion. Let's see what we can find."

"Wait for me, I'll go too. Someone could be trespassing." Sue Ellen ran inside to call her boss.

I grabbed bottles of water from the ice chest in the back of the van and gave one to Sue Ellen and one to Dan. Sue Ellen knotted up her long blonde hair, put on her red cowboy hat and stuffed her hair inside the hat. We three began walking to the cabins that were in the back of the compound. All the while we heard the bagpipes. As undeniable and far- fetched as it was, we were searching for the sounds. I tried my best to hold on to my composure. I was fighting a losing battle. All sorts of things were racing through my mind.

Was this really a sign of some sort? Had one of the kids had an accident? Had there been a plane crash? Why was I thinking bad things? Why. couldn't I relax and look for the good. Look for the bridge. Let it be good. I am crazy for sure. Please Neil.

As we were walking toward the cabins, a golf cart with two older men came driving our way. They stopped and introduced themselves as guests staying in one of the back cottages.

One of them said, "We've been driving around looking for the bagpipe music. Do you folks know where it is coming from? We've been around the road behind Eagle's Nest Mountain. The music sounded louder there, but then it sounded like it was coming this way. We decided to come to headquarters and see what you knew, Sue Ellen."

Sue Ellen said, "I don't know but these folks are

looking for someone called Neil. Didn't you say he
played the bagpipes, Mrs. Galloway?"

Dan looked at me. I looked at her. Dan wouldn't
open his mouth to help me. We knew Sue Ellen had
no idea Neil was our departed son. No need to explain
more than necessary to Sue Ellen, I said,

"No, Neil is our son. He's not here. But he sends
bagpipers to us sometimes. It's our first family reunion
and our anniversary celebration. I just thought he
might have sent one to help us celebrate." I felt faint.
I leaned on Dan and began to fight back my tears.
There was an old oak tree near, one with large
branches that reached to the ground. I walked over
to it and lifted myself on the lowest branch. Everyone
followed to find a little shade.

We had all gathered under the oak, listening.
The old men in the cart were laughing and having a
wonderful time. Sue Ellen was looking at Dan and me.
She had to be considering what our group would
be like.

Dan came over and sat by me. The music was still
playing. By this time, hearing as many pipers as I had
heard throughout the years, I knew bagpipers had
strong lungs and could play for long periods of time.

Then, the music stopped for a minute or two and began up again. It sounded nearer.

Suddenly, we all saw him! He was dressed in jeans and had on a baseball cap. He was walking very slowly down from the hill and continued to play. When he saw us, he stopped. I jumped up and ran to him as fast as my aching legs would take me. Stumbling along, I had no idea I could move so fast. I looked back at Dan and saw everyone watching in amazement.

"Marion, slow down. He'll be there." Dan, as he left to follow me, turned to the others in the group and said, "She has a particular interest in bagpipe players."

He was tall, taller than any of the others. And he was younger, I thought. He was handsome. Well groomed, short hair and no beard. He could have passed for a stockbroker or some important businessman. *Maybe he is visiting from Houston and innocently practicing his instrument on the hillside. Did anyone have a reasonable explanation?*

Not me. I wanted to know all about him and I wanted to know if there was any connection at all to the other bagpipers I'd seen in Texas. I think I frightened him because he immediately began to tell me why he was there.

He said, "I hope I haven't been bothering you folks. I didn't mean to cause any trouble. My secretary told me it would be okay to come out here to practice. She said she knew the owners and they wouldn't care if I played on the other side of the hill. She said no one could hear me there. I guess she was wrong. You see, my secretary asked me to stop playing in the parking lot in town because some of the merchants were complaining. I haven't had any place to practice so it was nice to know this place was available."

I asked, "Is this the first time you have been here on this place?"

"Yes, ma'am, it is. I thought it would be okay. I need to practice. I am new to the instrument. It takes lots of practice to master the pipes."

"Oh, it's perfectly okay with me," I answered. "I'm very attracted to bagpipe music. It is more than a little important to our family and me. If you don't mind me asking, where are you from?"

He answered, "I just moved to the area. I took a new job here."

I had to ask, "Are you an attorney?"

He smiled and said, "Hardly."

I guess he could see my disappointment. I didn't

quite know how to ask another question and Dan had hold of my arm.

"Come on, Marion, let the man go. It's too hot to be out here."

I couldn't be dissuaded. "Well, we are from Houston. Came out here for a family reunion and to celebrate our anniversary."

"What part of Houston? I moved here from there." He was an extremely friendly young man. Like the lawyer we'd seen.

"We live out west of the city," I told him.

"Small world, I lived out west, too."

I was no nearer a real connection except that he was a bagpiper.

Might as well get on with it, Marion. Find out if there is a connection to Neil.

"Well, what brought you all the way to the Hill Country?"

Dan was interested, too, but he didn't want the others to know. He stood a little behind me and, though he tried not to show his disbelief, I could see wonder in his wide blue eyes. I knew he didn't want to believe that the bagpipers were an all-the-time and everywhere thing. No doubt about it, this was not a coincidence. I asked for more information. I continued to search, "Not many young men are fortunate enough to get an assignment in this part of Texas. How did you manage?"

Then!

The young man said, "I'm the new funeral director out here. I was transferred from my job in Houston."

Somehow I knew. I asked, "Where did you work?"

"I worked at Memorial Gardens."

I almost gasped but held the emotion in. I told him Memorial Gardens was where our son was buried.

The bagpiper, knowing what to say, offered proper condolences.

I wanted to hug the young man's neck but restrained myself. I quietly said, "Thank you. You are a wonderful piper and I know you will enjoy your new-found music." It was almost too much, once again. I wondered how Dan was reacting and knew we'd need to talk.

Soon we began to disperse our little band of bagpipe searchers. Sue Ellen headed back to the dining hall and the men in the golf cart drove to their cabin. Dan and I lingered a minute or two. Lost in the moment.

Check in time was near. Close enough that if the manager had come to work, we could make our rounds to see the cabins before the family arrived. Dan and I walked like zombies in the heat of the noonday sun back to the registration desk. The manager was there and had registered all of our cabins. We signed, granting permission for each family to charge their snacks and gift shop items on our credit card. Our desire was to have everything ready for the family; all they'd need to do was drive to the parking lot near their cabin, unload and enjoy the days ahead.

The piper's appearance was something that happened before the others arrived and I wondered why. Maybe Dan and I had to experience the astonishing fact that Neil had been sending us reminders of his plans and he wanted to reveal his evidence once more before we told the family.

Dan and I unloaded our supplies before the others arrived. We'd reserved the largest cabin for ourselves because the little grandchildren were looking forward to sleeping over at our cabin. While I set up the kitchen and snacks, Dan filled the ice chests with soft drinks. After all was done, we were ready for the gathering of our clan. We were also ready to have a serious talk.

I began, "We'd promised we'd no longer ignore the wondrous happenings in our lives. Extraordinary as it seems, we've continued to experience the exact things Neil said he would try to make appear in our lives. These happenings haven't been illusions, Dan, nor have they come from mediums or clairvoyants. Neil has reached out to us and we've seen with our eyes and heard with our ears the sights and sounds he'd said he'd send."

"I know Marion, there's not a doubt in my mind about all of this but I don't understand any of it."

"I don't understand and yet I do, Dan. These aren't ordinary things that Neil thought about. Maybe they were. I don't know either. I only know that what is happening is real."

"Do you ever feel it'd be best to just go along our ways and not pay attention? I wish I understood." Dan was in a quiet mood and red-eyed again. He'd not been the same since we'd lost Neil. It seemed to me the older we get, the harder it got. Wonders or not, we missed Neil tremendously and had no thoughts of ever feeling differently.

"I know, Dan, and it isn't easy for me either. When

I'd tried to tell anyone, I'd felt like a kook so many times. Some kind of charlatan, even. But I know that's not true because all of the events are true. It is unbelievable but true. The only explanation can be is that Neil had these plans and he's doing all he can do to get through to us. He thought God gave everyone the powers to reach beyond their earthly limits. He wanted us to share in his experiments. I'm not sure how to explain what happens. I hope that if I keep trying to write the novel, Neil will continue to help me. I do believe God will help us."

It wasn't as easy for Dan's scientific mind. On the other hand, Neil was sending his important wisdom to us jointly – together. We'd been open and aware. The bagpipers, the songs, the written words, wonders in nature and all Neil had planned to try to send to us had happened and continued to appear. I wanted to make plans to tell the family. Rather than easier, our situation was becoming a dilemma.

I continued talking to Dan, "It was what Neil wanted us to do. Tell the rest of the family, his wife and children, he would always be with them. Neil told me about the bagpipers when he'd said, 'And at very significant times when there can be no doubt of something important, I'll send you bagpipes.' He promised serendipitous feelings in writing and mystical messages heard through music. Signs in nature. Everything happened and continues to happen. There's no doubt he's shown us undeniable signs of the bridge he's been building. He's here, with us. In all the ways he'd planned. My question is what made his plan possible for us?"

Pondering on the wonders of life and death, Dan and I agreed to wait until the last days of our celebrations to broach the subjects we'd been discussing. If all went well, we'd tell the family about our magnificent moments and of the plans Neil had wanted them to know about. We were concerned that the timing might not be right and that the children might not be old enough yet. The last thing we wanted to do was alienate any of our group. We would play it by ear.

The days passed swiftly and our family activities were filled with happy times. The food was western fare. Early morning chuck wagon breakfasts, cooked on grills outside, and delicious smells of sizzling bacon and eggs. Evening meals smelled of barbequed meats and sauces, chili, pecan pies and chocolate chip cookies.

We roasted marshmallows, placed them on graham crackers and drizzled melted chocolate over them as we sat around a campfire, listening to a strolling musician pickin' cowboy songs we knew. There were nightly sing-alongs. The ranch daily itineraries looked better than the best summer camps for children. Our family took it all in. Dan and I celebrated our anniversary in true Five-Star Texas dude ranch style.

The family gathered together on our last night, the children sat near their cabins where they'd built a huge bonfire. Circled around the fire, they sang songs and ate leftovers from the farewell dinner prepared by the ranch staff and served by Sue Ellen.

The closer we neared the time when Dan and I had planned to share our mystical experiences of the last years, the more difficult it seemed it would be. I didn't think Dan would bring up the subject, I knew I'd need to do much of it without help from him.

Feeling the stress and even a pain in my heart, I went away by myself after dinner and found the old oak tree where we saw the bagpiper coming from the hill on our first day at the ranch. I sat on the low limb and stared at the Eagle's Nest Mountain and quietly asked for help.

The words came with the breeze, "*Don't tell them yet Mom, you must write about it. Write, so they will understand. You'll be my Ghostwriter and I'll be your Muse.*"

And from the Professor, "*You must complete the book, Ma-ri-on Mau-reign. You must continue. You must go to your Muse.*"

And I remembered, over and over again, the books written by our teachers. The music and the messages in the songs. The signs in nature, the rays of light, the rainbows and the important surprise visits from the bagpipers. I sat in silence until I dreamily became aware again.

My memories drifted away as I strained to listen to a slight movement in the wooded area just in front of me. I could hear something breathing and moving on a tiny trail between the trees. Appearing in a shadowy moonlight that was shining on the oak tree leaves, a visitor came into sight. There he was, another deer. He looked like the one in Scotland. And the one near Nettie's house.

He was a young buck with a small rack of horns. I stood slowly and quietly – I wanted to acknowledge him. He stood still and gazed at me as I smiled at him.

It looked as if he smiled back. He held my gaze for a few seconds before he disappeared with no sound.

At that moment I felt the deer had jogged something loose in my thoughts, some sort of strange message. It seemed I was in balance again. I instinctively knew I would need to encourage the others to look for their individual answers. Dan and I couldn't explain our miracles and the things that had happened to us. When the novel is complete, some will question and, in questioning, some will find answers. That's how it began and that's how it should end: questioning the great secrets of life and the hereafter.

I made my way back to the group and found Dan. I motioned for him to follow me to the cabin. The others were still at the campfire, singing and enjoying their last night together.

I said to Dan, "I've come to the realization we don't need to explain anything about Neil and our experiences to the family. When we go home I'll complete the novel about building a bridge from eternity. My Muse will help. It will be right if I stay focused on the bridge and the events that happened while I've been writing about it."

"I'm glad, Marion. I didn't know how we could get our miracles across to them. It seemed to me we would need to build another bridge just to make them see what we've come to know and see."

Dan was his rational self. My wise confidant and my solid foundation.

We were primed to say more but we were interrupted.

We heard the porch planks squeak and a knock at the door. Dan walked to turn on the lights and I went to see if the grandchildren were returning to our cabin. I opened the door and froze in place. The handsome young bagpiper was back. He was dressed in kilts, the like of which I'd never imagined. Beautiful for sure; however, more wonderful than that. His kilt was made of fabric featuring the Texas state flower, the bluebonnet.

"Hello, Mrs. Galloway. I've been thinking you might like a little bagpipe music to celebrate your anniversary. I wanted to put on my new Texas kilt so I decided to come see you and your family. Is it okay?"

Dumbstruck, I muttered. "Come in. Sure, you can play for us. We'll get everyone together. They'll be as happy as we are. You are giving us a wonderful

anniversary gift."

"Yes, ma'am. I wanted to do that. I was surprised to find folks who like the pipes out here in this part of the country."

Nothing could have been more out of place, and yet so perfectly in place as we led the bagpiper to our family group.

I announced, "Listen up everyone. Grandpa Dan and I met this young man the first day we were here. He surprised us by coming back to show off his new kilt and play the bagpipes for us."

The three youngest children climbed in Austin's lap as he put his arm around his wife. Neil's and Heather's two teenaged children looked on with interest while Heather settled in a lawn chair near them. Travis and his wife sat close. Our first-born granddaughters – now in their 20's, beautiful and all grown up – sat together on the swing that hung from an oak tree. Dan and I sat next to my daddy's widow on the steps of one of the cabins and we listened to the sounds by the light of a full moon. A gathering of our clan had been called to hear the incredible music, so atypical for a dude ranch in the Texas Hill Country.

Our family group sat in rapture as the young man walked among us and played. Special to each of us, only Dan and I knew the importance of the event. That night Neil's entire family was gathered for the first time since his memorial service. They didn't know they were sharing an incredible love message sent to them from a wonderful spirit who'd been building a bridge from eternity, especially to and for them.

Neil had known the right place and time to send his message. The group was not aware at the time, but Dan and I knew it would be forever stamped in their memory. Maybe they'd read about it in a book one day, remembering all the long-gone members of the clan and thanking God for the great wonders that would certainly continue to appear in their lives. The key would be awareness to the miracle of love.

The young man bowed at the completion of his concert. It was a bow I'd learned to know and cherish. We clapped our hands and tried to show our appreciation. Then, our bagpiper slowly turned and walked through the oak trees into a moonlit night. We thought he had finished playing but as he disappeared, he began one final tune. The music was Robert Burns'

"Auld Lang Syne."

It was Labor Day in the Texas Hill Country and New Year's Eve memories flooded our hearts. I looked at Dan and he took my hand. We were crying tears of joy.

In Memory

Steven Patrick Westbrook
1955-1994

Maxine Moses Watkins
1915-2001

Pruett Watkins, M.D.
1913-2002

Acknowledgments

*Every one of my writings has been
furnished to me by a thousand different
persons, a thousand different things.*

– Wolfgang Von Goethe

My husband Bill, my loving companion, alpha and omega, in
everything we are together. Mama and Daddy did not live to see the
book published. They encouraged me, read and critiqued while they
could. I read to them when they couldn't. They set high standards.
They taught me to love music, books and nature. They taught me to
love, period. They started it all. Janice, Daddy's widow, is my friend
and constant support. Whenever she could, she filled in as she
thought Daddy would want. She is first editor and advisor.

Our two sons, Bill II and Doug always stand by me. Daily calls kept
my spirits up and made me think I could complete this book. I think
they can do anything they set their minds and hearts to do. I am
proud of them beyond words.

Our daughters–in-law, Susan, Ginger and Lisa, were positive and
loving readers, editors, supporters, advisors. Exceptional mothers
and wives, they are beautiful in every sense of the word.

Our seven grandchildren are delightful blessings and our pride and
joy. We're so fortunate to talk books, music and nature. And to share
our hobby of hanging out in bookstores. All my love to Jennifer, Liz,
Christopher, Katie, Aaron, Daniel and Abigail. You keep my heart
and mind young.

The Rev. Howard and Diane Caesar are our source in Unity. More
than ministers, teachers,and friends, they are dear extended family.
Thank you Howard and Diane for presenting Bill and me with more
opportunities than we'd ever dreamed possible. You changed our lives.

Cindy Cline-Flores is an earth angel to whom I send love and thanks.

Others of faith who helped shape my beliefs are: The Rev. Holland B. and Jane Clark, The Rev. Dr. Linda Watkins (my dear sister and family genealogist), The Revs. Sig and Janie Paulson, Father Leo Booth, Father Ron Roth, Rabbi Howard Trusch and The Rev. George Parrigin.

A novice writer, I found a world community of professionals joined in love of writing to be my teachers. My education began with a remarkable man from India, Venkatesh Srinivas Kulkarni (1945-1998), revered novel writing professor at Rice University. He was a part of this world for too short a while. Awesome friend, teacher and mentor to our son and me. To my supportive Kulkarni Rice University writers group, my deepest appreciation. We continue to meet: writers, authors and editors, Marjorie Arsht, Kathryn Brown, Judith Finkle, Bob Hargrove, Elizabeth Hueben, Karen Meinardus, Linda Jacobs, Joan Romans. More Rice writing friends—Winston Derden, Tonja Koeppel, Jeff Theall, Kay Walker, Diana Wade and Kathy Appelt. We share wondrous memories of the Professor.

Dr. Elizabeth Harper Neeld, expert in so many areas, she is a gifted teacher, many times author, speaker, wise advisor and balanced, gentle, graced-filled friend. Her loss helped me through my loss.

Texas writer Leon Hale, master of the short story essay and my teacher unaware, is inspiration personified. My days are brightened when I read his column.

Thanks to all at the Maui Writers Retreats and Conferences. I think it is the best place in the world to associate with the writing industry. It was Dan Millman who, in 1998, encouraged me to submit my manuscript to the writers retreat. More than the Peaceful Warrior, Dan exemplifies all he was created to be. Author, speaker, mentor, wise friend and thoughtful caring citizen of the world.

My first Maui teacher, Professor of English at the University of Hawaii, author Dr. Steven Goldsberry had confidence in me and taught me to get beyond despair. Steve has retained his interest in my book. Gloria Kempton, my second year teacher at Maui Retreat, is a cherished advisor, editor, online teacher, and good friend. Among the Maui faculty, visiting agents, editors, writers who consulted with me and/or encouraged me to keep writing are Cynthia Black, Patti Breitman, Terry Brooks, Richard Paul Evans, Kimberly Cameron, Robert C. Vines, Rosalie Grace Heacock, Jillian Manus, Chris Vogler, Lane Zachary, Jandy Nelson, John Saul, Jack Canfield, Tad Bartimus, Bud Gardner, Sam Horn, Dan Poynter, Laurie Liss and Bryce Courtenay. Thank you.`

Thanks to Whidbey Island Conference and the early attendees writers' groups. Another lovely island filled with encouragement. I especially thank those not mentioned above: agent Rita Rosenkratz, attorney/agent Jeff Kleinman, and editor Brenda Copeland, three of the nicest folks one could hope to find at a writers conference. Thanks to Texas Coalition of Authors and Ft. Bend Writers League for their hard work for all writers.

My important group of significant readers: author Guy and Pat, Charlie and Lynn, Jay and Charlotte, Revs. Barbara and Gene, Mike, Rev. Dan and Kathy, Marjorie, Bill, Jose, Syd, Charles, Aaron, author Dr. Pam, Winston, Maree and Bob, Jack and Karen, Bill and Vicki, Aron and Terri, Liz and Karen, and Dr. Barbara P. Beyond friendship and going to the limits for me are Guy (my understanding advisor), Michel (my sister in my heart), Lilly R., Amy Jane, Maybell (my wordsmith) and Jim, Bob and Rose, Carolyn and Fred, Jack and Millicent, Steve P., Elsie and Bill, Ian and Becky, Terry, Barbara Z., Paula, Betty Flo, Dr. Art and Delores, Dr. Earl and Nona, Dr. Jerry and Shirley, Dr. Warren and Dorothey, Harold and Dorothy, Barbara P., Tex and Nancy, Kathleen and Mike, Andy and Mike, Jean, Janette and C.A., Fulton and Edith, Linda, Martha and Alberto, Enrique and Gilma, Kurt and Marilyn, Carmelo and Hilary, Jo and Raja, B, Chowdhry, Bob and Marge, Mac and Janie (loyal friends of Steve and his family).

Our LOParkway, Cat Spring and Colorado County neighbors.

Special families with whom we share deep loss are: Art and Delores, Ed and Marie, Jeanette and Allen, Wilborn and Carol, Peggy and Joe, Carolyn and Fred, Joyce, Wade and Blanche, Tom, Margaret Sue, Erle and Kathy, Beth and George, Jean and Kenneth, Bill and Elnora.

Last minute editors, my special friends Donna Reinbolt, Aaron Ellisor and Vicki Barber. You saved the day. You saved the book.

Thank you Al Vacek, Lars Sloan, John H., HFD Bagpipe and Drums, HPD Bagpipe Band, important pipers all.

Thanks also to John Mason, Robert Burns Cottage Supervisor, Alloway, Scotland; Don G. Campbell - *The Mozart Effect*™, author, musician, speaker; Stephen L. Fiske - *Bridges of Love*, musician, songwriter, speaker, producer.

The men who made this book graphically beautiful own The Marion Group. Aaron Ellisor's inspiration is surely from his great Inner Source. He understood the project and loved it from the first day. Aaron and Charles Freeman lead a team of one of the best professional graphics and marketing companies known. Their work has made the book a success in my heart. The detailed, inspired care they gave to the cover, illustrations, layout, and printing adds to the story. Thanks to everyone in The Marion Group for seeing this project to the finish and for pushing me when I felt I couldn't go on.

BRIDGES OF LOVE

If we can reach so far
To send men up to the moon and rockets to the stars
Why have we been so far apart?
Why can't we find a way from soul to soul, from heart to heart?

Bridges of steel reach from shore to shore
Bridges of love reach so much more
They link our common hopes, our common ground
Joining one and all, the whole world 'round

We can all build bridges of love each day
With our eyes, our smiles, our touch
With our will to find a way
There is no distance we cannot span
The vision is in our hearts, the power is in our hands

For now more than ever
What the world needs more of
Is to reach for each other
With bridges of love.

(an excerpt)

Permission from Stephen Longfellow Fiske
© Fiske / Jai-Jo Music 1983